THE SILVER PENCIL

Janet Laidlaw lived in Trinidad, but the books she read took her all over the world—especially to America. No matter where she went in her imagination, though, Janet was sure that she would never leave the West Indies and her family's "House on the Hill." There, using the special silver pencil her father had given her, Janet wrote all sorts of plays and stories.

Mr. Laidlaw's tragic death changed that world forever. Before she knew it, Janet was in school in England. And after that, she chose to live in America, where she hoped to find both her life's work and a home of her own. Throughout it all, Janet used her silver pencil to turn her life into stories—and those stories began her career as an author.

ALICE DALGLIESH (1893–1979), whose life was the basis for this book, was the first children's book editor at Charles Scribner's Sons and the author of a number of award-winning books.

KATHERINE MILHOUS won the Caldecott Medal in 1951 for *The Egg Tree*.

The Silver Pencil

BY ALICE DALGLIESH

DECORATIONS BY
KATHERINE MILHOUS

PUFFIN BOOKS

THE SILVER PENCIL

PUFFIN BOOKS
Published by the Penguin Group
Viking Penguin, a division of Penguin Books USA Inc.,
375 Hudson Street, New York, New York 10014, U.S.A.
Penguin Books Ltd, 27 Wrights Lane, London W8 5TZ, England
Penguin Books Australia Ltd, Ringwood, Victoria, Australia
Penguin Books Canada Ltd, 10 Alcorn Avenue, Toronto, Ontario, Canada M4V 3B2
Penguin Books (N.Z.) Ltd, 182–190 Wairau Road, Auckland 10, New Zealand

Penguin Books Ltd, Registered Offices: Harmondsworth, Middlesex, England

First published in the United States of America by The Scribner Press, 1944
Published in Puffin Books, 1991
10
Copyright © Alice Dalgliesh, 1944
All rights reserved

Library of Congress Catalog Card Number: 91-52565
ISBN 0-14-034792-5

Printed in the United States of America
Set in Baskerville

AUTHOR'S NOTE

THIS BOOK is fiction and the characters are fictitious, with the exception of certain public figures and Professor Patty Smith Hill, whose name is used by permission. Many of the experiences of Janet Laidlaw are similar to my own; all the episodes in which children appear are true to life.

I am most grateful to the friends who read the manuscript, especially to Anne Carroll Moore and Louise Seaman Bechtel who gave me encouragement and many valuable suggestions.

The poem *Of Wounds and Sore Defeat* is from THE FIREBRINGER by William Vaughn Moody and is used by permission of Houghton Mifflin. *Leisure* by W. H. Davies is used by permission of Jonathan Cape. The lines from William Butler Yeats' poem are used by permission of the Macmillan Company.

ALICE DALGLIESH

To

my cousin

E L I Z A B E T H

in her sixteenth year

Part 1

HOUSE ON THE HILL

HOUSE ON THE HILL

Chapter
1

HOUSE ON THE HILL

THE GROUND was parched and cracked, the grass was burnt the color of straw. The leaves on the trees crackled with dryness, whispered eerily as the trade winds blew through the branches. Those persistent winds never seemed to cease blowing in this season of the year. At the street hydrants long lines of Negro women stood patiently, buckets in hands, waiting their turn. The feet of the children who clung to their mothers' skirts were white with dust. The whole earth seemed to be searching feverishly for water.

On the gallery of the House on the Hill, Janet Laidlaw stood looking up at the sky. For weeks—months—it had been the intense blue of a tropical sky in the dry season. Clouds, if they came, had grown discouraged and had drifted away. But now the sky was filled with enormous dark clouds that threatened and promised. And, as Janet stood there, the first drops of rain began to fall. Slowly at first, big drops that splashed and spread. Then sharper, pelting drops until the rain was a sheet of silver, a curtain hiding the world, a million pattering feet on the tin roof of the house.

"Mother!" Janet called. "The rain!"

Mother came out onto the gallery and watched the silver

sheet sweeping across the garden. "Thank goodness!" she said. "I thought that in another day we would have no garden at all. The rain beats down the plants, but when the sun comes out they'll lift their heads again."

Janet wrinkled her nose as she sniffed the freshness that rose from the earth. Only once a year could one smell that particular freshness. "But, Mother, what shall I do today?" It was always that way on the first days of the rainy season. After the rain had come every day for a month, one grew used to it. But the first days of imprisonment were restless ones. Today was Saturday and there was no school.

Mother considered. "You can always read."

"But I've read all my books."

"Then I have a new one for you." Mother went into the house and was soon back with a fat, brown-covered book in her hand. Janet took it with the eagerness with which she always approached a new book, and read its title.

"*Little Women*. What a dull name!"

"But not a dull book," Mother said. "It's a particularly good story about an American family."

An American family! Janet looked the book over more cautiously than before. She would have preferred the family to be British, like her own. Still, she would try the first chapter. Lying flat on the floor, she opened the book. It began with Christmas —so much to the good. And, after the first few pages, the rain was entirely forgotten—she was in America with Meg and Jo, Beth and Amy. That she would really be there some day, sharing their country, she did not know. At the present *they* were sharing *her* world, the small but vivid world of the tropical island of Trinidad. They were with her, sheltered from the storm, in the safe comfort of the House on the Hill. The rain drew its silver curtain closer around them. Janet read on.

The house was a long, low white one, built halfway up the side of a hill. The Laidlaws had gone there when Janet was nine years old. Up to that time life had been sometimes dull and sometimes fun, but, so it seemed to her later, life did not really start until she went to live on the Hill. At least everything that she remembered before that was a little gray and fuzzy around the edges, while memories of the Hill had a lovely color and they were so clear that thinking of them was like looking into a crystal bowl.

Janet hadn't been excited when she heard they were to move. They had moved seven times in nine years. Mother liked changes, and, as there had been so many moves, so many new houses, another one didn't matter very much. When the day came, Mother was calm and pale and limp, a little apart from all that was going on, letting Father do everything and being perfectly sure that the effort of moving would bring on one of those illnesses that she almost enjoyed. Father was anxious and worried about her, which suited her very well indeed.

At last everything was packed. Sweating Negroes piled the boxes and the furniture onto small carts drawn by thin, unwilling mules. The carts started off in procession. From crates on the last one came a series of high-pitched cackles; Janet felt a stir of sympathy as she watched the hens push their heads hysterically between the bars. They were all there, her own particular ones among them. That shrill, nervous squawk belonged to Queen Alexandra. The plump hen with the ruffled feathers was Victoria Regina. And the rooster, stretching his shining russet neck above the others, was Gustavus Adolphus Rex. Janet adored names, she savored them as another child might the hard, sweet brittleness of barley sugar. They rolled easily off her tongue, so all her pets were named in this high-sounding way.

With a final shout of protest from Gustavus, the last cart rattled out of the driveway, and Janet turned to look at Mother, sitting on the steps beside her, waiting for the cab to come. How pale she was and how unfamiliar in a hat! Mother never wore a hat, for she was so often ill that she never went out.

Father came down the steps and called Janet aside, his small yellow moustache bristling nervously, the laughter-crinkles quite gone from his eyes.

"Now, Janet, remember that Mother must be kept calm. When we get to the house you must be quiet. The servants have gone on and, by the time we get there, they will have some of the furniture in the rooms."

And Janet, who wouldn't have dreamed of being noisy, anyway, nodded solemnly. She had been through crises like this before and she understood Father perfectly.

The cab came and Father helped Mother into it, gently, carefully as if she were some fragile piece of china. Mother made the most of the occasion and sank gracefully into the seat, paler than ever. Father helped Janet in and took his place. The cab started with a jerk, its ungreased wheels whining a protest. Mother felt in her bag for her bottle of smelling-salts; crude sounds or smells always upset her.

The journey was not a long one and the streets were familiar. Most of them were bordered by small houses, their gardens bright with tropical flowers. In the poorer streets were the wooden hovels in which the colored people lived, each sad little house drawing around it like an outer garment the warm scarlet of hibiscus or the waxen glory of jasmin and frangipani. As the cab rolled along, children playing in the gutter stopped to stare at it. One small, black boy, naked save for a hat of bright green felt, stuck out his tongue. Janet would have liked to return the greeting, but, she decided, it might be disturbing to Mother.

Now they had come to the market, a large red-roofed place in the center of town. The color which overflowed it seemed to leap and quiver in the sunlight. Negro women in bright cotton dresses and turbans sat by their carefully arranged trays of vegetables. Red of pepper, pale green of christophine, orange of pumpkin called enticingly to the passer-by. Among the stalls, East Indian women moved with grace and music in their white *saris* and tinkling bracelets.

In the gutters *corbeaux,* small, evil vultures, pecked at the decaying vegetables. Janet looked at them. One repulsive old grandfather stared back at her, then seemed to wink with a beady eye. Mother saw it too, and shuddered, holding the smelling-salts to her nose. To her the market was all dirt and odor; to Janet it was color and life and interest, with the acrid, unpleasant smells only a part of the enchanting design.

As Mother shuddered and closed her eyes, Father leaned over her anxiously. "Here is the driveway!" He could not, of course, conceal the fact that the market was exactly across the way from the approach to the new house, so he might as well get it over quickly.

Mother opened her eyes and smiled faintly. She wasn't missing anything—not even that to the right was Coffee Street, where

5

the East Indian colony lived. That meant tom-toms when there were weddings—very disturbing. She sighed and leaned back against the seat.

The driveway was a long one and the angle was steep. The old horse went slowly, more slowly, patches of sweat staining its thin flanks. Janet wondered if it would be able to get up the hill, and wished she could get out and walk. She was excited now, for all this through which they were driving was theirs—acres of land, not just a tiny garden such as they had had at the old house. She tried to see everything as the horse plodded slowly along; green ferns bordering the road, an old cocoa tree heavy with pods of pink and maroon, delicate lacework of bamboos against the sky. Then they turned a corner sharply, and the house came in sight.

It was a comfortable house that looked as if it had been there, as Janet thought, for a million years. It could never have been new; never have been built. No, it had simply sprung up amid the growth of the hillside and, because it had not been lived in for a while, the Hill had almost taken the house to itself. Strangely enough, in all the wildness of the creeping, smothering, tropical undergrowth, the house sat prim and serene like a lacy valentine. It was built in the French tradition of the island, with a long open gallery overdecorated with wooden scroll work. Above the gallery and the windows, a coralita vine hung its delicate, heart-shaped flowers. In the garden, begonias still carried on a feeble, losing battle against the weeds.

The cab drew up by the front steps. Father got out and gave Mother his hand. She put her foot carefully on the bottom step, then drew back. "John!"

On the third step was a snake, coiling itself into the air, waving vaguely to and fro. As they watched it, the unwelcome brown body slithered across the step and was gone.

Mother was clinging to Father's arm, and he was saying, "It's all right, darling. Just a harmless whip snake. There's a lot of bush around the house, but we'll have it cleared in no time."

They went up the steps. Unnerved by the snake, Mother went at once to her room and sat, stiffly resigned, on the one chair that had been unpacked. But Janet ran delightedly, brimming with curiosity, from room to room. As she went she talked to herself, for every one was busy and there was no one else to talk to: "Look at this big pink room! And a yellow one! This little green one must be mine. I want it, anyway, because the coralita vine looks in the window."

Still talking to herself, Janet came to the drawing room; stopped and drew a long breath. She had never seen a room just like it—dark and cool, panelled in cedar. So large, so empty, and so entirely without friendliness, for as yet no furniture had been put in place. Janet shivered and hurried through the doorway onto the gallery, where the sunlight lay in warm, golden pools.

From the gallery the Hill seemed to drop away, abruptly. The town of San Fernando lay far below, the red roof of the market making one splash of color among the roofs of corrugated tin. Beyond the roofs and the streets was the sea, beyond that the dim outlines of the mountains of Venezuela. To the south stretched fields of sugar cane. The tall canes were in arrow, the wind racing through the flower tassels until they seemed a rippling, tawny sea. Blue sea and gold sea; it was hard to tell which was the lovelier.

Janet stepped back into the cool darkness of the drawing room. This time she was not alone. In the center of the polished floor sat a gray mouse, eying her curiously. She made another step forward, and he scurried into a hole in the panelling.

It was pleasant to have company in the big bare room. "I shall call him MacGregor," decided Janet. "MacGregor the Mouse. I hope he will come back again."

Father came in just as the tip of MacGregor's tail disappeared. He was looking more worried than ever.

"We've forgotten something," he said. "Pussy!"

"Goodness!" said Janet. "We'll have to go back and get him." For Pussy, a severe and cross tom, who didn't look in the least like his soft name, was an important member of the family. Then it was her turn to look worried.

"But MacGregor! How will Pussy and MacGregor get on?"

"I haven't the least idea who MacGregor is," said Father, a little impatiently, "but whoever he is, he'll *have* to get on with Pussy."

"It's the other way round—because you see MacGregor is a mouse."

Father laughed, then, and put his arm around her.

"You're such a funny thing," he said, kissing her lightly on the tip of her nose. "Of course we'll see to it that MacGregor's interests are taken care of, though it may be a bit difficult to explain things to Pussy."

Janet laughed, too, and rubbed her cheek against his coat sleeve. Now the big room was no longer empty, but filled with friendliness and understanding.

"It's a nice house, Father. I'm going to love it."

"Yes," Father said. "And do your best to make Mother love it? She has had a bad start!"

Chapter 2

THE FIRST DAYS in the new house were uneventful. After the effort of seeing the furniture put in place and the curtains hung, Mother was exhausted and stayed in bed. The servants, quite accustomed to this, carried on the household routine. Fat black Caroline bustled about the kitchen, a separate building some distance from the house, chuckling approval of the spacious kingdom that was now hers. Her happiness bubbled over into the making of sugar cakes, confections of coconut and brown sugar. Janet found them, in all their spicy fragrance, cooling on a banana leaf by the kitchen window.

In and about the house the servants were busy, too. Dark unreliable Maud waited on table and sang as she swished the dishes in cold, soapy water. Thin yellow Rachel, cross as two sticks, but with a passion for cleanliness that was Mother's joy, looked after the bedrooms. In the garden, Moses-and-Aaron cut back the bush that had almost swallowed it up. Aaron, an East Indian coolie, was the gardener, but on certain days of the week he drank too much rum and his brother Moses showed up to take his place. As the brothers were much alike, and no one was ever quite sure which one of them was there, the family simply called them, collectively or singly, Moses-and-Aaron.

While Mother was in bed, Janet sat beside her daily, giving

bulletins of all that was going on, helping her, she hoped, to like this beautiful new home. "There's a mouse in the drawing room, oh, a very *clean* mouse named MacGregor. No, Pussy hasn't bothered him. And there are lizards on the gallery. I touched one and his tail dropped off. It wriggled. There are wonderful little green paths that go up the Hill, I've been exploring and I got my hair full of burrs. Maud combed them out. No, I didn't see any snakes. And there's a big bunch of bananas on the tree in the back yard. Caroline says we'd better pick it before the birds get it."

Whether all this was reassuring or not, Mother decided that she would get up and see things for herself. After a week or so she felt sufficiently recovered to have guests for dinner. Not many guests, just a friend of Father's and his wife, with a visiting American who had come to the island to collect specimens of butterflies. It was quite an event, however, for Mother seldom thought she was strong enough for company. Janet loved dinner parties and it was she who arranged the centerpiece of fern and coralita, standing back, head cocked on one side, to admire the effect that it made with the lamplight shining softly on it. Every now and then a beetle flew in through the twilight and buzzed feverishly against the shade of the lamp. Janet caught it in her hand and threw it out of the window, at which it promptly buzzed back and was thrown out again.

Dinner went smoothly. Janet did not say a word, for she was so interested in the tall, friendly American and the way he ate. It was her first experience with some one from a country whose ways and customs were different from her own. Almost all the time he held his fork in his right hand, which, Janet had been taught, was very bad manners. What he did with it fascinated her so that she surreptitiously put her own knife at the side of the plate and experimented. The peas fell off the fork and some of them rolled across the tablecloth. A frown from Mother made her pick up her knife hastily. Taking her eyes from the stranger for a moment, she tried to listen politely to the conversation.

"No, indeed," Mother was saying. "You don't know what it is to be in a house that hasn't been lived in for five years—and that's right in the bush. Ants! Cockroaches! Lizards that run right under your feet! We've killed two centipedes and a scorpion."

"But there hasn't been anything for a whole week," Father added. "We're really getting quite civilized. I had Moses-and-Aaron cut the bush right back to the Hill and——"

He did not finish his sentence. Maud came rushing into the dining room, the picture of terror, her eyes showing white against her dark face. She stood, opening and shutting her mouth like a fish, twisting her apron in her fingers.

"Maud!" It was Mother's voice with a thin edge of ice in it.

"Madam!" Speech came back to Maud and flowed from her like a torrent. "A snake, madam! A snake in my pantry! I see it with my own eyes. As Jesus is my witness, it dance on my pantry table!"

"Nonsense," said Mother. "Snakes don't dance."

But Father rose from his chair. "That's our whip snake again! They don't dance, but they *do* rise on their tails and sway to and fro. I'll go down to the pantry with you, Maud."

"I'll go along," said the American. "I'm useful with bugs and snakes and things."

By the time the men and Maud had gone down to the basement pantry, the snake had disappeared into a hole in the wall. But for a week he kept Maud in a state of terror. Sometimes the whole of him appeared in the pantry and once again he "danced" on the table. Sometimes it was his head that came out of the hole on the outside of the wall and looked inquiringly around, forked tongue going in and out. A snake's head appearing and disappearing like that was too much for Maud. She gave notice. Mother was upset, too. There were too many creatures around the house, she said; she couldn't stand them—especially the ants that ran about the floors at night.

So, one afternoon, Father took his gun and waited grimly for the snake's head to appear on the outside of the wall. Moses-and-Aaron, puttering around the garden, shook his head over it.

"No good shoot snake's head off," he said. "Snake come back —look for head—bite you."

But at that moment out came the snake's head, and in and out went the forked tongue. Father fired. The snake's head was gone—blown into a hundred bits; the body hung limply from the hole. *That* was disposed of. Now for the ants!

That night when Janet was in bed, safely tucked under the mosquito net, she heard a soft plop, plop, on the floor of her room. Cautiously, with her nose pressed against the netting, she leaned forward to see what it was. The moonlight made a bright patch on the floor and in that patch sat a large toad— *crapeaud* in the French patois of the island. He sat very still and looked at her.

"Father!" shrieked Janet. "Father!"

Very sleepy, his hair rumpled, Father came into the room. "Janet! What is it, darling? Another nightmare?"

Janet pointed to the patch of moonlight. "A *crapeaud* in my room!"

Father laughed. He untucked the mosquito net and sat down on the edge of the bed.

"Never mind the *crapeaud!* He's a friend and I invited him in. He eats ants. If he stays in your room ants won't bite you. Go to sleep now and don't worry."

Then he tucked her up again and the *crapeaud* stayed. Janet grew quite used to his plop, plop, in the night. The ants went and Mother decided that the house was not so bad, after all. If they could only get rid of the lizards that hid behind the pictures in the drawing room, she wouldn't move. But these were not the pretty little green lizards that ran about the gallery, nor the big ones in flashing rainbow colors that lived in the garden. These were large lizards of an unattractive putty-gray that made one shiver to look at them. Maud's sketchy dusting did little, so Rachel was invited to help. The lizards fled before her energetic cleaning and the cockroaches in the pantry found another home.

Only MacGregor remained, through Janet's special pleading, for Mother was not fond of mice and Rachel's broom itched to sweep him out. No one knew why Pussy let him live, but there seemed to be a sort of armed truce between them. With the undesirable creatures gone, the family drew a breath of relief for it *was* a nice house and they wanted to stay in it.

Then came The Night. They always spoke of it like that— with capital letters—The Night.

Chapter
3
RED SKY AT NIGHT

ALL HER LIFE Janet remembered that night. She had gone to bed early, but somehow she did not go to sleep. There was a strange light in the sky, but that was not exactly what kept her awake. Nor was it the shrill cry of the cicadas, nor the soft plop, plop of the *crapeaud* that kept guard in her room. After a time she heard Father and Mother go to bed. But Janet lay there in the darkness, watching that dull red glow in the sky, wondering vaguely about it, sensing the unusual feel of the air.

Then it came! First a series of muffled explosions, far off, like the sound of cannon. There followed a series of rumbles; distant, frightening. The sky glowed from one end to another, deep blood-red. The soft velvety darkness that the windows usually framed had become two squares of red, like fiery eyes looking in at Janet. Terrified, she jumped out of bed and ran into the next room.

Mother and Father were sitting up in bed. Father held out his arms and Janet rushed into them, hiding her face on his shoulder.

"Steady, there," he said. "We must see what it is."

They went out onto the gallery and looked down on the town. Over the sea hung the crimson curtain of the sky. The dull rumblings continued; the muffled explosions came at intervals. The town had come to life. People were running out into the streets in their nightclothes, looking up at the sky. Some of them fell on their knees and bits of confused, frightened prayer drifted up the Hill.

"They think the end of the world has come," said Father.

Janet clung to his arm. "Has it? Oh, Father, has it? Are we all going up to Heaven like Elijah in the chariot of fire?"

Father patted her hand. "No, it isn't the end of the world, at least not for us. It's a volcanic eruption. I saw the Soufrière was threatening and I'm afraid the eruption has begun. But the Soufrière is in St. Vincent, miles away. It can't hurt us here."

That was Father. Whether it was ants or a *crapeaud* in the night, or a volcano, it was safe when he was around. The only time he ever got excited was when Mother was ill—and then he became a different person.

The sky was still red, the rumblings kept up, but at last every one went back to bed. For days after that the polished tops of the tables were covered with gray volcanic dust, and there were dull rumblings and mutterings, but the sky did not flame again. Both the Soufrière in St. Vincent and Mont Pelée in Martinique were in eruption. Mont Pelée had wiped out the whole town of St. Pierre. The curious sulphuric smell in the air and the gray dust filled Janet with awe, for they had brought death with them. She looked up at the Hill with a new respect. It was not very high, but it was shaped like a volcano and at any moment she expected it to burst into flame.

Life wasn't always as exciting as that. For a long time it went along in a quiet routine. Janet went to a small private school. It was a one-room school and there were three tables, covered with black oilcloth. Janet sat at the middle table with other children of her own age. Sybil and Enid, her two best friends;

Geoffrey, who lived in the house below hers on the Hill; William, bursting with plumpness and always falling asleep over his books. She loved school, but only certain parts of it. There were times when it seemed beautiful and thrilling. Those were the times when they did not have arithmetic, when they read Shakespeare aloud or wrote compositions. Composition filled Janet with delight. While Enid and Geoffrey and William sighed over "Honesty" or "Humor" or "Patriotism," and scrunched themselves painfully over blank sheets of paper, Janet took the bit in her teeth and galloped into the topic.

"Patriotism," she wrote, "is loving your country and maybe dying for it. I love Trinidad because I was born here. I love England, which is my mother's country, and Scotland, which is my father's country. Norwegians and Swedes love their countries. But for me to love it, a country would have to be British."

There were horrible hours spent learning the dates of all the English kings and queens in the long, dreary stretch from William the Conqueror to Edward the Seventh. Dates were the only dull part of history, the rest of it was a joy. For then the four walls of the schoolroom stretched outward—outward—and one could ride to the Crusades with Richard Coeur-de-Leon or thrill over the deeds of Edward, the Black Prince. And the history of Trinidad, with Columbus naming it after the Trinity, was best of all. That was not in any book. Miss Johnson, their young teacher, told it to them as a story—they hung on her words, even fat William kept awake, listening as avidly as the rest.

That day, when Janet went home from school, she went out onto the gallery and looked out across the sea. There, in the waters of their own Gulf, Columbus' ship had lain at anchor.

There Indians had gone out in canoes to meet the Men from Heaven. There, with the great mountains in plain sight, Columbus had failed to know that he had found a continent.

Little shivers ran up and down Janet's spine. History in a book, history of faraway countries was one thing; history that had happened, as it were, on one's doorstep, was another. It had caught and held her imagination. She hurried into her room, found a piece of paper and a pencil and began to write. The pencil rushed over the paper, slowed down, crossed out words, rushed again. Then it stopped. Janet read aloud the words it had written; they sounded perfectly unfamiliar to her. Mother? No, Mother had a headache. Still in a frenzy of excitement, she ran downstairs to the pantry, where Maud was working and singing loudly as she worked.

"Maud!" Janet shouted, balancing precariously on the pantry window sill. "I've written a poem!"

"What yo' say, Mis' Janet?"

"A *poem*, Maud. Listen!" and Janet read:

Sailing, sailing, sailing, over the boundless sea
Sailing the ship has been, and months have passed drearily,
And now a figure kneeling on the deck is heard to pray,
"O, Father, in Thy mercy, to land show us the way."

Janet took a breath, and Maud, always glad of an excuse to delay her work, sat down, her dark face completely without expression. Janet went on:

If to save our lives it is willed by Thee,
The Land shall be called the Trinity.
Columbus rose, his faith was great
And he trusted that starvation was not to be his fate.

Emotion and the effort of getting that very long line into one breath completely overbalanced her, and she fell into the pantry. Landing on her feet, she went on, with scarcely a break:

Oh, joy, "Land, land in sight!" they cry.
"We are saved, we are saved, we are not to die."
And before any nearer to the island-gift they came,
Reverently Columbus pronounced its name,
"La Trinidad," and lo! as they drew near,
The sailors gazed with awe, perhaps with fear.

("The best part is coming, Maud. Listen carefully.")

Three peaks they saw, the Trinity those three did represent,
And one and all felt that they knew what the mystic wonder
meant.
Trinidad, that island, a wonderful gift from on High,
Was a token of how Heaven answered a man's despairing cry,
And she has ever prospered and ever won renown,
For the island of Columbus is the flower of England's crown.

"It do sound good," said Maud, returning to her dishes. Janet waited a moment, with all a poet's hopefulness, but a second reading was not requested. Feeling a trifle flat, she went back to her room and read the poem over to Pussy, who yawned widely.

Now Janet could hardly wait for Father to come home. Indeed, she was halfway down the drive to meet him, the paper clutched in a moist hand. "Father! I've written a poem!"

Father smiled and hugged her. "Give me a chance to get in the house, Jan. It's hot!"

Time dragged until Father had had his bath and a cold drink and they were sitting out on the gallery. It was, of course, the perfect setting for the poem, with the Andes across the water. Father read the poem over without smiling, then looked at Janet as if seeing her for the first time. "Fine. Where did you get it?"

"Out of my head. Is it a good poem, Father? Please tell me —is it?"

"It's a good poem for a little girl. But where did you get this 'flower of England's crown'?"

"Out of a book," confessed Janet. "It was a little pink guide-book and it said, 'Jamaica is the Pearl of the Antilles, but Trini-dad is the fairest flower in England's crown.' Nice, isn't it?"

Choking slightly over his drink, Father said, "Very nice. And I think if you've words like that you're ready for grown-up books. Let's see what's in the bookcase."

Together they went to the tall bookcase in the dining room where books in leather bindings sat in state behind the glass doors.

"Walter Scott—any of his," said Father. "And Thackeray, maybe *The Rose and the Ring.*"

"I—I've read most of them already," Janet said. "On rainy days I get them out. I've read *Pendennis,* at least parts of it."

Father laughed. "Then you're ahead of me! The books are yours."

"But do you think I'm going to be able to write poetry, Father?" asked Janet. "Real poetry like *The Lady of the Lake* or Tennyson?"

"Well, hardly," said Father. "But if you keep on writing, maybe some day you'll write *something.* I don't believe you're going to be a Scott or a Tennyson! Keep on with your reading —collect words but don't copy other people's combinations of them. Make your own!"

And so, on rainy days, Janet read Thackeray and Scott and went back to the friendly bookshelf in her own room where she could look at the lovely Kate Greenaway pictures for *Marigold Garden* and read *Little Women* for the fiftieth time. There was, too, the book of Norse myths that she loved, with its stirring tales and the never-to-be forgotten picture of Thor's struggle with the Asgard snake. *Alice in Wonderland* was a special favorite because of the pictures of the heroine. Janet had found out, through study of herself in the mirror, that she was not at all pretty. Rather nice blue eyes, to be sure, but an up-tilted nose, freckles, a mouth that was too wide. And the hair! Straight as straw and much the same color; hopeless until one pushed it back relentlessly with a round comb, or tied it back with a ribbon. And then—why, then one looked something like Alice in Wonderland. To be like her was interesting and made up in some measure for not being pretty. That was why the blue covers of *Alice* were worn and almost falling apart— though not by any means the only reason.

Chapter
4 BROTHERS ARE LIKE THAT

MOTHER WASN'T ALWAYS BUSY being ill, and in-between, she paid a great deal of attention to Janet. She listened to her stories and read aloud to her and told her about England. Father told stories, too. They were of Scotland and the sheep farm on which he had grown up. Gradually, Janet made patterns in her mind, a pattern for each of the countries she had not seen. The pattern of England was one of green fields with hedges full of blackberries, and flowers whose names had come to be as familiar to her as her own, but none of which she had seen, except in pictures. The pattern of Scotland was of gray stone walls, of shepherds sitting around the fire and of heather on the hills. Heather she knew because it came, flat but fragrant, in letters from Scotland.

There was another picture, vague in detail, that was America, the country where the Little Women, Meg and Beth, Jo and Amy, lived, and that produced the monthly *Ladies' Home Journal*. In America there were mysterious things like pickled limes, and little girls wore enormous bows of ribbon on their hair.

Thinking of these countries made her have the same feeling that she had on Christmas morning—with a pile of exciting packages to be opened. Some day she would see the blackberry hedges and heather hills with her own eyes. America—that wasn't a "belonging" country, but a strange one out of a story book. Meg and Jo and Beth and Amy could live there if they wanted to, but for herself it didn't matter if she ever saw America.

Then Lawrence came home and with him came the whole wide world. For Lawrence had gone around the world in a sailing ship and had a great deal to say about it. Now Valparaiso and Rio, New York and Canton ceased to be small black dots on the map and settled down cozily in the Laidlaws' back yard.

It was an adventure in itself to meet a nineteen-year-old brother for the first time. Lawrence was ten years older than Janet and when she was born he was at school in Scotland.

Then he had run away to sea, and, finding it harder than he expected, had come home to help Father in the drygoods business, as a dutiful Scottish son should.

Yes, it was exciting to have a grown-up brother. Janet circled around him cautiously and he eyed her with as much caution. Then, one was not sure how, the ice was broken and they were walking hand-in-hand along the streets, as Janet proudly showed her brother the town.

Brother! It was a wonderful word. Janet said it over and over to herself. She said it aloud at school and at play, dragging it into the conversation whenever she could. "My brother says," "My brother thinks." In the end, she so completely drenched Lawrence with sisterliness that he began to weary of the whole relationship. In fact he grew positively surly.

A Sunday morning in November set things right. They had walked to church with Father, soberly, as befitted a Presbyterian Sabbath. Janet, in white muslin and blue silk sash, tried hard to keep pace with Lawrence's long strides. Sitting beside him in the church pew, she thought how wonderful he was, and looked up at him lovingly. Lawrence colored up and looked away. Seeing that he didn't want to be stared at, she turned her attention to the Baker family.

In the long, dreary desert of the sermon, there was always the comfort provided by the Bakers. In the center of the church stood the small harmonium played by Mrs. Baker. Mr. Baker, who, like Father, was an elder of the church, sat directly behind the harmonium, with his family. There were ten young Bakers, one for each year, and all of the same shade—which was as dark as it was possible for a Negro family to be. Their clothes were as white as the angels'—though no angel's robe ever was so stiffly starched. The heads of the youngest children barely showed above the top of the pew. Each little girl had pigtails tied with white ribbons; each little boy had hair that curled so tightly as to leave bare spaces on his head. Occasionally a boy or girl would fall asleep, then Mr. Baker would lean over and administer a sharp tap on the head. Janet always expected, and hoped, that the little Baker would start singing "Twinkle, twinkle" like the Dormouse at the Mad Hatter's teaparty—but it never happened.

She admired the Bakers intensely. Now, to take her mind off the length of the sermon, she thought sadly of the time when, yearning to know them better, she had gone to Sunday School. The Bakers *were* Sunday School. In their white clothes and stiff, buttoned boots they sat in the front pew, with a few children of assorted brownish shades behind them. The whole Sunday School was filled with the triumphant darkness of the Bakers. Longing for friendship, Janet squeezed herself between Lily and Mignonette, the two nearest to her in age. The little girls looked at her with calm, unsmiling faces, then drew their starched skirts aside a trifle, and folded themselves in an atmosphere so chilly that Janet knew she would not get far with them. She did not go to Sunday School again.

As she thought, with pain, of this experience, the sermon ended and the minister gave out the number of the closing hymn. Janet opened her hymn book, rose with the congregation and climbed on a hassock. Elevation always seemed to help her singing.

"*Onward Christian so-ol-jers,*" she shrilled, in a somewhat tuneless voice, a heritage from Father, who recognized *God Save the King* only when other men removed their hats.

"Marching as to war!"

Lawrence gave her a poke. Mistaking it for applause, Janet sang even louder:

"With the cross of Jesus going on before—"

Lawrence gave her sash a violent tweak, which brought her down from the hassock, making noises like a music box running down.

"Shut up!" he hissed in her ear. "Shut up!"

Janet glared at him, but stopped singing. She would tell Father about it when they were walking home from church. Father *always* understood.

But this time he didn't. Indeed he laughed, quite heartlessly.

"Don't tell tales," he said. "Brothers are like that. Just be a good sport and learn to take it."

So it was that Lawrence ceased to be the eighth wonder of the world and the relationship simmered down to a brotherly-sisterly give-and-take, with real friendship still in the future.

Chapter 5

THE SILVER PENCIL

CHRISTMAS WAS DIFFERENT that year, because Lawrence was home. Janet was perfectly happy because she was no longer alone; there was a brother to share the day, even though he teased her and—still worse—ignored her for long periods of time.

On Christmas Eve, when every one, including Lawrence, was

full of good will, she was able to see to it that he hung his sock at the bottom of his bed. More hopeful for herself, she hung up a pillowcase. In the very early morning she awoke and felt it cautiously, but it was still limp—Mother and Father had not been in. She slipped out of bed and tiptoed to Lawrence's room to tuck into his sock the beautiful, magnificent present she had selected for him. It was a large china mug with LOVE THE GIVER in gilt letters amid pink flowers.

In the morning the pillowcase still hung limp, and Janet, scarcely able to believe her eyes, had the same all-gone feeling that had come the year she said good-bye to her belief in Santa Claus. Mother and Father *couldn't* have forgotten. She dressed hastily and went out into the dining room.

The family was at the table, having early morning coffee. Lawrence was drinking his, she noticed, gratefully, from the china mug. She went around the table kissing Mother and Father, hesitating when she came to Lawrence, who did not like to be kissed—at least not by her.

"Merry Christmas, darling!"

"Merry Christmas!"

Lawrence looked at her owlishly over the top of the mug. "Merry Christmas, kid!" but he didn't offer to kiss her. Apparently the mug had not, after all, delivered its Christmas message.

Janet sat down by her glass of milk. Father leaned over and put two teaspoons of coffee into it—that was a special treat. She sipped the milk, slowly. Surely some one would say something about that dreadful, flat pillowcase. But no one did. The milk almost choked her, she could scarcely swallow.

Breakfast over, they went into the drawing room. And then

Janet knew that the pillowcase hadn't meant anything at all, that no one had forgotten. For against the dark panelling shone the green branches of a stiff little Christmas tree. It was the first she had seen, fir trees being rare in the tropics, even artificial ones like this. It was glittering and lovely, with colored balls and waxen angels and silver trumpets. She stood looking at it in complete silence.

Father, who had sent to Germany for the tree, looked as if all his Christmas plans had come tumbling down like a house of cards. "Don't you like it, Jan? We thought it would be fun to have our presents this way." He indicated the pile of presents near the tree.

"I *love* it," Janet said solemnly. She went nearer to the tree and touched a silver trumpet with a caressing finger. "It is the most beautiful thing I've seen in my whole life."

Father beamed proudly. "There! I knew you'd like it."

Janet was still touching angels and balls and trumpets, to make sure they were real. The pink and gold angels swayed as she touched them and seemed to fly among the branches; enchantment was in the faint tinkle of the bells.

"It's a Christmas tree, isn't it? Like the one in Hans Andersen's story?"

"It's a Christmas tree," agreed Father. "And look what is on the very top of it."

Janet looked up. Close to the star was a silver pencil, something she had wanted for a long time. Father took it from the tree and put it in her hand. It was smooth and cool to the touch.

"For your stories," he said. His fingers went to his vest pocket, where, even now, one of the stories was safely tucked.

He carried the little stories around with him and read them proudly to his friends, but Janet did not know this.

"Oh, Father!" she said. "Thank you! I'll always and always write my stories with it, even when I'm an old lady."

"Not too many promises," said Father. "Some day it may be a fountain pen. Now let's open our parcels. You first, of course."

Janet stretched out her hand to take a package, but drew it back as the sound of drums and fifes and voices came from the yard.

"It's the Christmas singers. Oh, Father, don't let them come in!" She couldn't tell why they terrified her so, except that they were masked, as at Carnival time, and some of them walked on stilts. The deep, Negro voices rolled out on the air:

It came upon a midnight clear
That glorious song of old,
From angels bending near the earth
To touch their harps of gold.

There followed the snow-clad verses of King Wenceslas, inappropriate in the warm sunshine, and the pagan rhythm of a Carnival song:

Oh, poor me one! poor me one!

Then Father gave the men pennies and they went away and one could settle down to the parcels again. Janet opened a very small one. It proved to be a tiny, leather-covered Bible, with her initials in gold on it—just the thing to carry to church on Sundays. The card said it was from Mrs. Wilson, the minister's wife.

Janet registered mild approval and waited patiently while Mother opened a parcel, and Father opened one, and Lawrence one. Then she chose a bigger package that looked bookish. There were several books she hoped to get.

The tissue paper fell back to show another Bible, a larger, sturdier one with "To Janet with love from Father" on the fly-leaf. Janet swallowed her disappointment hastily and smiled gratefully. "Oh, Father, what a nice, *big* Bible! I can use this one at school."

"That's what I thought," said Father, relieved.

Again the round of parcels, and again a large, bookish one for Janet. This time her fingers shook as she turned back the paper. It must be—it had to be—the *Swiss Family Robinson*. Why, every one knew she had wanted that for *ages*. It *had* to be.

But it wasn't. When the last layer of paper was removed it was a Bible, another and larger Bible, with a stiff, hard cover. It had come all the way from Scotland, for the fly-leaf said, "To our dear little granddaughter from Grandfather and Grandmother." And pressed between the title page and the first chapter of Genesis was a sprig of heather.

Janet stared down at the Bible, her lips trembling. She could feel the tears stinging her eyes. Then she looked up and saw the slight quiver that Father's moustache always gave when he was trying hard not to laugh.

The tears hurried back where they had come from. Laughter bubbled up in their place.

"I—I'm bad sometimes," Janet gasped. "But not *that* bad! Not enough for *three* Bibles."

They were all laughing, now, and Christmas was fun, after all.

When the last package had been unwrapped, there was still the big wooden box that stood in a corner. This was from Uncle Jack, who had been on a business trip in America, and for days Janet had been longing to open it. Now Lawrence pried up the boards with a screwdriver and every one gathered around to see. When the box was open, Janet leaned over and took out the first shining red apple, held it in her hands, sniffed its fragrance. For years the sharp, cidery tang of apples would mean America—even if, as later, they were English apples. The fruit was exciting in itself, but, more thrilling still, each apple was wrapped in American Sunday comics.

Not even stopping to bite into her apple, Janet took the bright, crumpled pages, smoothed them out carefully and lay flat on the floor to read them. They had to do with the antics of Buster Brown, a small boy with square-cut hair, and his dog Tige. Lucky American children who could follow Buster from week to week! Tantalizing to get him to a certain spot and have to leave him there for ever.

To console herself, she took a crunchy bite of apple. Then she was aware that MacGregor the mouse had come out and was sitting nearby, watching her with bright beady eyes. MacGregor by this time had grown very tame, and would even eat from Janet's hand. She bit off a piece of apple and held it out. MacGregor nibbled daintily at it, approved, and scurried with it to his home in the wall.

Late that evening, when the wax candles on the Christmas tree were lighted, Pussy came stealing, tiger-like, through the half darkness, a limp object in his mouth. Janet gave a sharp little cry, for it was MacGregor. The long truce was over.

Chapter
6

THE SILVER PENCIL was a miracle. It was handsome to look at, delightful to use because it never needed sharpening. One had only to change the lead. Janet was sure that she could write almost anything with it. Confidently she sat down at her small table, with clean sheets of paper in front of her and the shining pencil in her hand. To her surprise, exactly nothing happened. The paper remained blank and white, for not a single idea came into her head. It was as if that perfect tool, the silver pencil, had, with its small red rubber tip, erased all imagination.

Actually nothing of the kind had happened. Janet was simply finding it difficult to write because she was the only child in her circle of friends who had that particular kind of imagination—and while imagination flourishes alone and in secret, it also craves fellowship. Geoffrey, who lived in the house just below hers, had imagination but it was entirely scientific—he was always puttering with "inventions." He and Janet could meet on common ground only over the mechanical toys they both loved—small ships that rocked, when wound, in circles over imaginary waves, trains that ran also in circles, ducks that quacked and waddled realistically. As soon as Geoff soared off on flights of inventiveness and Janet talked of fairy tales and of magic, they were as far apart as air and water.

Then there was Sybil, Janet's closest friend, who was an explorer and tomboy by nature and regarded books with distaste. Many hours she and Janet explored the green paths that led up the hill, pushing aside bushes and tangled vines. There was always something that Janet hoped to find; she imagined this was an impenetrable jungle. To Sybil it was just the Hill and bushes to be pushed out of the way.

Enid, the "second-best friend," was feminine and loved romance. She had a single-track mind, so she and Janet played endlessly at being a young couple eloping from a stern father —a game by which Janet soon found herself extremely bored, but which she went on playing because of affection for Enid.

So imagination, not stimulated except by books, wasn't taking Janet anywhere at all. Her writing was something that set her apart from her friends, not something she could share. It was likely that the silver pencil would have been tucked into a corner of the table drawer if the need for writing a play had not come along.

Janet and most of her friends subscribed to an English magazine known as *Little Folks,* a patronizing name which they accepted meekly and uncomplainingly as they did the even more absurd name of their other magazine—*Our Darlings*. The subscribers of *Little Folks* supported by their contributions a children's ward in a London hospital, and it was for this worthy cause that Janet and her friends decided to give a play.

The great idea burst upon them one day when they were all at Enid's. A play, of course, but *what* play? There they came up against a blank wall, for not one of them had a suggestion. They looked through books but found no plays. Then it was that Janet rather timidly suggested, "Perhaps I could write a play? Do you think I could?"

The very thing! They rallied to her, gathered around her, all talking at once, all offering suggestions. At last she had found a kind of writing in which one was not entirely alone! But she found it difficult to suit every one, to handle all the suggestions.

"It must have Romance"—from Enid, of course.

"It should be about a great invention," from Geoffrey.

William, a pudgy, solid boy, thought it should be funny, because he loved puns and was always making unsuccessful jokes.

Her head awhirl with all the suggestions, and feeling her responsibility deeply, Janet went home. Once again the silver pencil and the clean sheet of paper. This time she began at once to write.

Beginnings were fine but got nowhere. Ten lines of an untitled play beginning—with alarming abruptness, "I love you. Will you marry me?" for Enid. Five lines of a feebler one named *The Secret of the Jungle* for Sybil. Nothing but the title of *The Great Inventor* for Geoffrey, because here Janet was entirely out of her depth. Not even a beginning for William. And at last they all went in the wastebasket.

In the end, she pleased herself and produced a tolerable, if rather thin play called *The Queen of Hearts,* which, miraculously enough, pleased everybody. They rehearsed it at Enid's house, which had a big bay window at the end of the living room, making a natural stage. It wasn't hard to assign the parts, for Janet had almost unconsciously kept her friends' characteristics in mind as she wrote. Enid was, of course, the Queen of Hearts. There was even a part for William—naturally he was the Court Jester. And Geoffrey was the one who mixed the mysterious potion that made the Queen fall in love with the Jester. It wasn't a very original plot, but to them it glittered with newness. Janet herself was too shy to take a part, besides she was author and stage manager; that was enough. At the end of the play, she knew, there was often a call for "Author." That would be her moment, she would only have to walk onto the stage and bow. If she had to act in the play, she would die of fright. She admired the cool way in which Enid and Sybil went through their parts, and wondered how they could do it.

One week before the play, came that bleak, unbelievable morning when Father did not wake up. Although he was still a comparatively young man, his heart had been giving trouble, and on that particular night it quietly stopped beating.

The morning was full of confusion, with people hurrying to and fro, hurrying softly in the stillness that lay over the household. All kinds of people came to offer help and sympathy; people Janet and her family had never seen, but to whom Father had been kind. On the back doorstep, an old East Indian woman sat and rocked to and fro. Father had helped Mrs. Rupee to find her husband when he deserted her, and now nothing would persuade her to leave.

"Good sahib gone! Good sahib gone!" she moaned over and over again. She was like a thin white-wrapped wraith, putting into words all the unhappiness that lay between the four walls of the house. "Good sahib gone!" Her voice rose in a high, keening wail.

The funeral was held that same day, as most funerals in the tropics are. By noon Janet was a very miserable little girl, but no one had much time for her. Lawrence wandered about, pale and tight-lipped. Mother was in bed, worn out with weeping. Janet didn't cry, for to her everything seemed so dreamlike and unreal. That *couldn't* be Father who lay so still. Father never lay still. When five o'clock came, she would walk down the driveway to meet him and he would laugh—no, he wouldn't, because he was dead, people said he was dead. To her he only looked as if he were asleep.

"Wouldn't you like to go home with me for a little while?" asked the minister's wife, who had come to help. Janet decided that she would, for she loved going to the Manse, and it would not be so full of sadness. At least Mrs. Rupee wouldn't be rocking on the doorstep and one could get away from the rhythm of her mournful chant.

So she went down with Mrs. Wilson to the Manse. A little of the heavy feeling of sadness stayed behind on the Hill, but most of it went with her. Her world—her bright-colored world —had suddenly turned gray. Green trees, flowers, the sky and the sunshine, all seemed overlaid with a gray mist—like the tables in the living room when they were covered with volcanic dust. Even the familiar and pleasant things in the Manse were gray. Janet stood it as long as she could, then the words overflowed.

"Every Sunday Mr. Wilson tells us God is love and God is kind," she said, her voice trembling. "But He *isn't,* because He has taken away my father. Other girls don't lose their fathers. Why do I have to?"

Mrs. Wilson put an arm around her gently. "Because each person's life is different," she said. "All of us have a share of sorrow—to some it comes a little sooner."

"It didn't have to come to *me*. Not so soon," Janet said, rebelliously. Then, flatly, *"I don't love God."*

Mrs. Wilson didn't answer this. She said in brisk tone, "Do

you want to help me arrange the flowers for the church? To-morrow's Sunday, you know. We have some of them in the pantry and Violet Baker is bringing some from their garden."

Janet did not feel in the least like arranging flowers but she followed Mrs. Wilson into the pantry. There were the big vases that always stood each side of the pulpit, and some smaller ones. Flowers floated in a pan of water. She had helped to ar-range the church flowers before, and knew just what to do.

"Cut their stems a little," said Mrs. Wilson, handing her a pair of scissors. "I'll get another vase."

Janet was still in her rebellious mood, but it softened as she took the flowers out of the pan and began to arrange them. Tall white lilies to stand proudly upright. Graceful trails of white coralita to cascade over the sides of the vases. Small pink hibiscus for color. The first vase as she finished it was so lovely that for a moment she forgot everything else. As she put the last hibiscus in place, she felt that some one was standing in the doorway. It was Violet Baker, her arms full of roses.

"I've brought the flowers," Violet said shyly and Janet sud-denly knew that the Bakers' unfriendliness had been due to shyness. She was shy, too, so she understand exactly how it was.

"Put them in the water," she said. "Mrs. Wilson will be here in a minute. Will you help me arrange them, Violet? Aren't they lovely!"

Solemnly, silently, the two little girls chose long-stemmed roses and put them in the vases. Not a word was said, but there was a satisfying feeling of companionship.

The vases were almost filled. Then, in the stillness of the late afternoon, came the sound of the church bell. It did not usually ring on week-day afternoons and for a moment Janet wondered what it could be. Then she knew that it was tolling—for her father's funeral. The tears that had not come before came now, and splashed on the flowers.

Violet stood and looked at her, pity welling up and the tears coming into her own eyes. She did not know what to say, yet something must be said.

"Your father was a good man. My father will miss him in the church." And, frightened by hearing herself say the sympathetic words, she hurried through the door, leaving Janet alone.

The bell was mournfully insistent. It seemed to echo Mrs. Rupee's chant. "Good sah-ib gone," in measured metallic tones. "Good sah-ib gone."

There was no need to keep the tears back, now. Janet put her head down on the table and sobbed. Mrs. Wilson came in quietly, put a handkerchief in her hand and went away again. The bell stopped tolling, but the tears still flowed.

In a few days the grayness passed and things began to look normal. God took His accustomed friendly place again and part of the heavy weight lifted from Janet's heart. It came back, of course, especially at the time in the afternoon when Father should have come home, but it stayed a shorter time each day. The darkest time was the night of the play. Janet had supposed that her life would go on as usual, that she would be there to see the play through. But Mother was horrified when she suggested it.

"How *can* you want to be in a play so soon?" she asked fretfully. "Children haven't any feelings."

"I'm not in the play," Janet said. "But I wrote it and I want so much to see it."

"It's out of the question," Mother said, and turned her face away.

So on the night of the play, Janet sat alone on the gallery, where she had so often sat with Father, and followed, in her mind, every moment of the production. She could see it all: Enid looking so proud and pretty in her Queen of Hearts costume, Geoffrey measuring out the potion in his too-careful way, fat William bursting out of his jester's suit and trying so hard to be funny, but never quite succeeding.

It was something very near to heartbreak.

Chapter 7

GOING "HOME"

THEY ALL TOOK UP their lives again where the thread had broken, but every one was a little different.

Janet was quieter, a little more within herself, because things she had told to Father now went without telling. Lawrence had become, overnight, a man, sharing the responsibility of the business with Father's partner. But the greatest change of all was in Mother. After a month or so in bed, entirely withdrawn from everything that was going on, she suddenly pulled herself together and walked—without hesitation—into life. She went out, now; she was the moving spirit of the household. She did the planning; as far as possible she took Father's place. Janet did not understand it at all.

The years that followed were years of routine, the family life going on, but nothing of any special interest happening. Then Mother decided that it was time for Janet to go to school in England. Almost all Colonial children went to England when they were twelve or thirteen. They spoke of it as "going home," though most of them had never set foot on English soil, because they had heard their parents speak of it that way.

The days of preparation broke the quiet pattern of living. They were busy and bustling ones. Clothes took up a great deal of the time, for Janet had to have a whole new wardrobe. Mother sent to England for lengths of flannel and blue serge; the flannel for dresses, the serge for a coat. Mrs. Roberts, the dressmaker, spent all her days at the house on the hill; the sewing machine clicked and whirred from morning until night.

When the clothes were finished, they were fascinating but strange. A dress of pale blue flannel, one of pale pink, one of white. The coat—that was the strangest of all, and how hot it was! But it had an anchor on the sleeve and magnificent, shining brass buttons.

"It seems hot, now," said Mother. "But you'll be glad of it even in the summertime in England. Three dresses won't go very far, as soon as we get there we'll go shopping." Could it be Mother who talked so energetically of shopping?

It wasn't easy for Janet to say good-bye to Lawrence, to Maud and Rachel, to Caroline and to all her friends. Pussy was included in the tearful farewells, though up to this time Janet had not quite forgiven the murderer of MacGregor.

The voyage was long and the first part of it was tiresome, for Janet was seasick; dreadfully, unpleasantly seasick. When at last she was able to sit on deck, she found herself beside a boy of about her own age. He was wrapped to the nose in a rug and two large, sad dark eyes looked at her over the rug's cheerful plaid. There was something about the eyes that reminded her of MacGregor the mouse, and they aroused in her the same protective feeling she had felt for MacGregor. The boy's thin hand lay on the arm of his chair and Janet wanted to lean over and put hers on it.

Boys had, up to this time, been very much a part of her life, good friends to play with—but this feeling was a little different. She knew, of course, that one couldn't suddenly take the hand of a perfectly strange boy to whom one had not even spoken. Her sense of humor, the lively sense of humor that was her best gift from Father, came to her rescue. She could imagine herself saying to the boy: "I just had to pat you, because you remind me of my pet mouse." And she giggled at the absurdity of it.

The black eyes blazed with startled surprise. Pushing down the folds of the rug, the boy sat up and looked at her.

"Are you laughing at *me*?"

"No," said Janet. "At myself."

"Oh. . . ." muttered the boy, dubiously. The sudden movement had made him a little sick again and he hurried back into the sheltering folds of the rug. From this refuge his eyes peered at Janet, more MacGregor-like than ever. She choked back the laughter.

"My name is Janet Laidlaw. What's yours?"

"Jacques," the boy said. "Jacques Leroy." She knew, then, that he belonged to one of the old French-Creole families. His slight accent should have told her that before.

"Where are you landing? Southampton?"

"No, Cherbourg. And I wish I were there now. The sea is horrible. Up and down it goes and takes my stomach with it."

Janet nodded. "I know how it is. Are you going over to school?"

The boy shook his head. "No, for my health. I am very nervous and they think the change will do me good. You see—" He threw off the rug again and sat up. "You see, I killed my little sister."

Janet shrank back into her chair. "You——"

"I killed my little sister." He seemed to take a dreary pleasure in repeating the words that fell on the air like small, sharp pieces of ice. "It was an accident, of course. Only she is dead—and she was very little and sweet. I don't know why I am telling you this—" He crept back into the rug again, confused, evidently expecting disapproval.

This time, without thinking what she should or should not do, Janet put a comforting hand on his. How cold his fingers were! In that moment she was not thirteen. Jacques was not thirteen. They had been talking together as grown-ups might talk.

"Don't speak about it, Jacques, if you don't want to. Don't if it hurts."

The black eyes blazed again. "It hurts and it doesn't. I don't know why I told it to you, I have not said anything to any one. I can't say any more—now."

"You don't need to," Janet said. Then, quickly, "Oh, look! There's a whale spouting!"

They threw off their rugs, raced to the rail. Everything else forgotten, they were children again, clinging to the rail, staring eagerly out to sea. The wind was salt on their lips, it blew Janet's hair against Jacques' cheek.

"Oh, there it is! What fun! Look, Jacques, there it blows again!"

After that the voyage did not seem so long, for she and Jacques were friends. There was a warmth and color to their friendship that was different from anything she had known. Jacques, she discovered, had lived, like herself, in an imaginative world of his own. They had liked the same books—with some differences because he was a boy and she a girl. Jacques, also, had tried to write; had experienced the same difficulties. Janet found herself telling him the story of her play and the awful disappointment of the production night.

With all the confidences that were exchanged, she never asked Jacques to tell her about his little sister. But one day he told her, in slow difficult words, told her about the gun that he had thought was not loaded. . . . It was particularly hard for Janet to listen, for her lively imagination instantly recreated the whole tragic scene. Once the story was told, the two of them raced, laughing, around the deck, glad of the sunshine and the sparkling of the sea, glad of the return to everyday things.

"I don't know what your girl does for my boy," Jacques' mother said to Janet's mother as they sat in their deck chairs and watched. "But she has done something that none of us has been able to do. She has made him laugh." Being French, she added smiling, "I think our children are a little in love."

"Oh, no," said Janet's English mother. "How perfectly absurd! Oh, *no*!"

It was as Janet and Jacques ran around the deck that they

fell over Julia, who was coming the other way. Julia, small, dark and partly Spanish, had been trying for days to make Jacques see her. He was the kind of boy she liked, she had decided, and she, why she was most certainly his kind of girl. Why, therefore, did he waste his time playing with that pale, snub-nosed English one? No, Julia was not at all sorry when they fell over her and stopped to apologize.

From that moment they were always three, not two. Julia seemed everlastingly to be at Jacques' elbow, looking up at him with warm, adoring eyes. Janet felt the comradeship that had been between her and Jacques melting away. For Julia's face was like a flower, her hair curled softly around it, and she had a Latin way with her that made Janet, in contrast, as stiffly English as a pink-and-white daisy.

When the ship steamed into Cherbourg harbor and the passengers crowded the rail for a glimpse of France, Julia was there with Jacques. Her brown eyes more liquid than ever, she was giving him some religious pictures. Jacques took the small, lace-edged saints into his hand and looked down at Julia, smiling. Between them lay the bond of their religion; Janet, watching, felt more out of it than ever.

When the tender came to take Jacques ashore—with Julia, whose family was also landing at Cherbourg—Janet was not there to see them go. She was down in her cabin, sitting on the edge of the berth, looking at a small, crumpled picture that Jacques had dropped. It was with difficulty that Mother persuaded her, a little later, to come up on deck and see, as they steamed across the Channel, the shore line of the Isle of Wight.

Part 2

BYWAYS IN BRITAIN

BYWAYS IN BRITAIN

Chapter
8 *PICTURES COME TRUE*

ENGLAND UNFOLDED before Janet's eyes like a picture-book. Even from the ship she could see the bright patchwork of fields separated from each other by what, she was sure, must be blackberry hedges. And when they landed it was a summer afternoon with big, fleecy clouds in a blue sky and long shadows on the grass. She wished that Jacques could see it with her; wondered if he could possibly find France as beautiful, was sure that he could not.

They went first to Grandfather's house in a Kentish town. There was something peculiarly solid, to eyes that had seen nothing but wooden buildings, about this square, red-brick house. The pages of the picture-book were turning so rapidly now that Janet could hardly keep up with them. Grandfather with his close-cut beard and stern mouth; Granny—her step-grandmother—friendly but remote; red-cheeked Lizzie, the maid, in her black dress and crisp white apron; the garden with all the flowers of *Marigold Garden* suddenly taking on their true size and color and fragrance, and fruit trees trained against warm, brick walls. The greatest delight was in smell. Tropical flowers were almost without fragrance, except for the heavy, cloying scent of jasmin and frangipani. Time and again Janet knelt on the grass and buried her nose in the border. Lavender she picked and kept in the pocket of her dress; that was a fragrance not to be parted with even for a moment.

Meal times also brought surprises and pleasures. They had tea in the garden the first afternoon, with Lizzie bringing out plates of thin bread-and-butter and slices of cake. At the end came bowls of ripe, red strawberries—new to sight and taste and smell—with a jug of thick cream to pour over them and sugar to sprinkle on top. All that spoiled the afternoon was a spreading stain of strawberry on a pale blue dress.

"She needs more practical clothes," Granny said, eying the stain. She had never quite approved of Mother's ways of thinking or of Mother's choices. "Blue serge." The way she snipped off the words made blue serge seem totally undesirable.

"I'm going to get her some when we go to London," Mother said.

"The sooner the better," snorted Granny. "More strawberries, child?"

Janet definitely did not care for Granny. But Grandfather, in spite of his stern looks, was different. He took her, on a summer morning, to Canterbury, a long drive through buttercup-golden fields to streets where old, old houses leaned crookedly against each other. Then through a gate to the gray cathedral in its gracious setting of velvet lawns and wide-spreading trees.

Here the pages of history came alive. It did not seem real to Janet that she was standing by the tomb of the Black Prince— that hero who had ridden so dashingly through her history book. He slept quietly, now. Above the tomb hung the black armor that soldiers had followed into battle.

As Janet and her grandfather stood there, the gray walls of the cathedral seemed to rise into endless space above them. Through periwinkle-blue windows the sunlight streamed, the filtered beams just missing the Prince's tomb. Janet had a sense of being very small, no bigger than the motes of dust that danced in the slanting sunlight, but she had, also, a sense of being very English. She belonged here, her mother's people had belonged here before that, her feet were on solid and familiar ground.

Grandfather, looking down at her intent face, must have sensed what she was feeling, for he put a hand on her shoulder. But, being English, he had no words for the occasion, and so said nothing at all. And being half English, Janet understood without words.

The rest of the summer was spent in a town on the coast of Cornwall, with all the cousins. The cousins had lived in Trinidad, but in a town forty miles from Janet, so she had not known them very well. Now they were all in England at boarding school.

There were two families of cousins. The Gordons, half Scottish like Janet, were so handsome that Janet never felt related to them. Nora, with dark eyes and fair hair, lovely blue-eyed Ellen, Murdoch, a scrubbed-looking little boy who was a cherub on Sundays in his Eton suit with its stiff white collar—they made Janet feel a changeling.

The boys of the other family, Frank and Gregory, were handsome, too. Only the girl, Evelyn, was a comfort to Janet. For she also had long straight hair and freckles, in fact there was a strong family resemblance between the cousins, with the general advantage on Evelyn's side.

They all got on well together that summer, handsome ones and ugly ducklings alike. With their three mothers, they stayed together in lodgings and spent long hours on the sands. The

Cornish beaches were made for children. White-capped waves broke on long sandy crescents, above which frowned cliffs, honeycombed with smugglers' caves. Here again the pages of the picture-book were turning swiftly. Janet found, in the fields outside the town, the blackberry hedges, and filled her handkerchief with the fruit. The ripe, purple juice stayed on the handkerchief always; the berries were made by Mrs. Bolten, their landlady, into blackberry-and-apple pie. A pie with flaky crust and purple juice oozing out of it—a pie topped with a white mountain of clotted cream. The boys smacked their lips loudly and appreciatively; the girls gave ladylike oh's and ah's.

But after all, while food was pleasant and undeniably important, the *most* important thing about Cornwall was meeting the Somervilles in the scarlet-rambler room.

One afternoon the cousins—all of them—had gone on a walking trip through Cornish lanes and villages. There was beauty every step of the way. Thatched cottages with their geranium-bright windows and pocket-handkerchief gardens; fields sprinkled with poppies and ox-eyed daisies; the haymakers busy in the warm sunshine; and, again, that peculiarly English pattern of light and shade on the grass. The air was filled with the indescribable sweetness of a summer day. It was good to be young and alive and walking through it.

They came at last to a long white cottage which advertised, on a swinging sign, the magic word TEA. Beneath it were the still more entrancing words SPLITS WITH CREAM. Splits were a kind of Cornish muffin. One split them, naturally, and spread the halves with a thick—oh, *very* thick—layer of clotted cream and strawberry jam, then bit into them with delight. The cousins' mouths watered as they thought of it.

"Let's stop here for tea," said Frank. "It's a good place."

Had they enough money? They compared notes. "I've got sixpence." "A shilling." "Two-and-six." The last a magnificent gesture from Nora, who, at sixteen, was beginning to think of her figure and buy fewer sweets. Between them all they could muster up enough money for tea and splits. There wouldn't be anything left, of course, but what did that matter? Only the present counted.

They knocked on the door, the shining brass knocker making a hollow sound that startled them. A rosy-cheeked woman opened the door, smiling. Cornish people were particularly smiley, or so it seemed.

"Tea?" she asked. "Go out into the garden and take one of the scarlet-runner rooms. I'll bring it to you there. Splits of course?"

"Splits!" they agreed in blissful chorus. "With jam."

The children were puzzled by "the scarlet runner rooms." They soon found out what was meant, for part of the garden was divided into small rooms by poles on which scarlet runner beans made a natural wall and a decoration with their gay flowers. The "single rooms" were all occupied, but there was one "double room" with two tables, one, fortunately, large enough for the seven cousins, with a chair left over.

They sat down, happily, noisily, and waited. At the other table was an attractive woman with two girls, one about twelve, the other a good deal younger.

Tea came and splits and strawberry jam—and wasps. The cousins weren't especially disturbed, strawberry jam and wasps seemed to belong together.

"Come out of there, you filthy little beast," said Gregory, fishing one out of the jam pot.

The wasps were equally busy at the other table. One lit on the plate of the younger girl, she screamed and ran to the protection of the cousins' table. There she sat herself down in the extra chair and regarded the boys and girls with interest. Obviously, this was what she had been dying to do, all along.

"We have wasps, too," remarked Murdoch, fishing another one out of the jam pot. He was not especially attracted to small girls somewhere near his own age.

The little girl sat where she was. Her mother rose and came over to the table. "Jean loves company," she said. "But, Jeannie, they haven't asked you to stay."

"But I am *going* to stay," announced Jean. Her large blue eyes were fixed so firmly on Murdoch that he wriggled and grew red from the collar up. He moved his chair over a trifle and turned his attention to another wasp in the jam pot.

"We come from India," Jean's mother said. "I've been listening to you talk and I'm sure you are Colonials, too."

Nora nodded. "From Trinidad."

"Then we've lots in common. Suppose we put the tables together?"

Jean gave Murdoch a triumphant glance and moved a little nearer to him.

The older girl, Moira, was shy, but sitting next to Janet, nearest to her in age, she began to talk. "Where are you going to school?" she asked.

"I don't know," Janet answered. "Mother hasn't decided. She hasn't even decided where we are going to live."

"We live in Wimbledon," Moira said. "It's near London. I go to Wimbledon Hill School, so does Jean. Wouldn't it be fun if you could go there, too?"

Janet agreed that it would. When tea was over they found that Mrs. Somerville and her two girls had lodgings just across the street from them in Newquay. By the end of the summer Janet and Moira were close friends. They went everywhere together, with Jean tagging after, like the tail of a kite. And Mrs. Laidlaw had agreed to consider the Wimbledon school. As soon as she and Janet left Cornwall they would look for a flat. Janet had never lived in a flat; it sounded exciting.

Chapter 9

WIMBLEDON HILL

"You'll like the school," Moira said. She and Janet and Jean were walking the mile to school, an uninteresting mile between rows of houses. They were next-door neighbors, now, for Janet and her mother had been fortunate enough to find a flat in the same house as the Somervilles.

All three girls wore the school uniform, blue serge box-pleated tunics with white blouses and green-and-white ties. The two older girls wore stiff-brimmed sailor hats. Jean's hat was mushroom-shaped because she was only a little girl. She looked very small but sturdy, as she trudged along with her school-bag over her shoulder.

"She has only one book," explained Moira. "But she *has* to have a bag like mine."

"I wish we were going to be in the same form," said Janet wistfully. A lonely feeling was creeping over her.

"We couldn't possibly be," Moira said quickly. "I'm only in Upper Third, and they'll put you in the Fourth, I'm sure."

"Then," Janet said, "there won't be a single girl I know."

"I don't know many girls in my form really *well*—only Phyllis and Kathleen," comforted Moira.

"Don't know—why?" The idea was strange to Janet. In Trinidad she had known *everybody*.

Moira laughed. "This is England," she said. "You don't know a whole lot of people here the way you do in India or Trinidad. But you know a few. Anyway, you know Jeannie and me, and if you know a few people really well, it's better than knowing a lot of people a little."

Janet was still weighing this remark in her mind when they turned in at the school gate. The building was of red brick, ivy-covered. Janet's knees shook.

"I'll take you to Miss Garner's office," said Moira, cheerfully. Before she knew it, Janet was there. Miss Garner, the head-mistress, was pleasant but she had cold eyes that went through one like a blue steel blade. Janet thought to herself: Why do headmistresses look like that? If ever I'm head I'll be a nice smiling one.

Miss Garner was speaking. "I think we'll start you in Lower Fourth," she said. "Colonial children are apt to be a bit back-ward in some of the subjects. Then, if you do well, you may have a double remove another year. Moira, take her up to Miss Archibald's room, will you?"

If it was bad meeting Miss Garner, it was worse going to the Lower Fourth. To walk into a room full of thirty blue-clad, strange girls—to have thirty strange pairs of eyes looking one over! But Miss Archibald had red hair and kind blue eyes and a nice smile. Her voice was pleasant, too.

"You may have the desk at the end of the front row, Janet," she said. Janet slipped thankfully into a desk near the door, and Moira, seeing her settled, went to her own room. A terrible feeling of aloneness came over Janet.

"You're new, aren't you?" The voice startled her and she turned to see who had spoken. The girl at the next desk was looking at her, questioningly. She was a small girl with an impish grin and a pointed face almost entirely covered with freckles.

"I'm Biddy," she said. "You must be Janet Laidlaw, the new girl Archie told us about. From India, aren't you?"

"West Indies."

"Oh—it's all the same—I knew it was one of the Colonies." Then in a whisper, "We've one other Colonial in the form. Jessie, over by the window, with the long, straight hair. Her father was governor of Ceylon and Jessie has never got over it. Your father isn't governor of anything, is he?"

"No," Janet said. "He wasn't." She wished this strange girl wouldn't talk about her father.

"Good!" said Biddy cheerfully. "I think we'll be friends. Oh, I say, Archie wants us to be quiet."

Miss Archibald's calm blue eyes looked over the group. "Ready, girls? There's the bell."

The Lower Fourth marched out of the room in double file and flowed down the hall like a long, blue river.

"Keep to the left going up or down stairs," whispered Biddy. "If you walk on the right or run in the halls it means a disorder mark."

"What's that?" Janet whispered.

"You'll find out if we talk much more," Biddy hissed.

They were down in the big assembly room, taking their

places among rows and rows of girls. In the Upper Third, Janet saw Moira's dark curls. There were no chairs, the girls stood or knelt on the floor as occasion demanded.

Now the mistresses were filing up onto the platform and the girls were starting the perfunctory sing-song that always began Prayers.

"Goo' morning, Miss Smith, Goo' morning, Miss Burke, Goo' morning, Miss Hughes-Hallett." So many mistresses! Janet wondered how she would ever learn their names.

Miss Garner came forward and held up her hand. The blue-clad ranks dropped to their knees. Janet listened to the soft rise and fall of their voices in a prayer unfamiliar to her. This was a Church of England school and the prayer was the Collect for Grace:

O Lord, our Heavenly Father, Almighty and Everlasting God, Who has safely brought us to the beginning of this day, defend us in the same with Thy mighty power and grant that this day we fall into no sin, neither run into any kind of danger. . . .

The prayer was over and the girls were on their feet again. Now they began the school hymn in Latin, their voices high and clear:

> *Veni, Sancte Spiritus*
> *Et emitte caelitus,*
> *Lucis tuae radium . . .*

There followed school notices, some of them meaningless to newcomers. Then the blue lines again formed in twos and flowed through the halls to their rooms.

It was all so different and Janet was homesick. But it was

pleasant in the Lower Fourth room with Archie's soft voice in the history lesson, and after a time Janet relaxed and felt more at ease. It was not so pleasant in the Latin room, where she found her Latin pronunciation not the approved one. Nor was it pleasant in algebra, the subject in which she was "backward."

Later she and Moira met in the playground.

"Like it?" asked Moira.

"Rather," answered Janet, cautiously.

One o'clock came and school was over for the day. Some girls stayed for luncheon and preparation, but Janet and Moira took their prep home. Moira's form was dismissed half an hour earlier, so Janet found herself walking home alone. She did not mind this, it gave her a chance to think over the crowded happenings of the day. Not far from school she realized that she was being followed. A pretty girl with curly red hair and one with short, straight yellow hair and a sharp unpleasant face were walking at her heels and giggling. At first Janet didn't connect the giggles with herself, and turned to share the fun. The giggles continued, and suddenly she had the sick feeling that they were laughing at *her*. She stood very still and looked at them defiantly.

"You're a Colonial, aren't you?" the red-haired girl asked.

"I'm from the West Indies," said Janet, with dignity. Both girls burst into loud laughter.

"A little Indian!" they giggled. "A wild Indian!"

Janet walked on rapidly, her face growing redder with each step. Fortunately, the girls lived about halfway between the school and her flat, so they soon left her, with a parting shot: "Good-bye, wild Indian!"

Janet was bursting with indignation. When she got home,

Moira was sitting on the low, board fence, waiting for her. She couldn't wait to tell of the indignity; her words tumbled over each other, they came so fast.

Moira was sympathetic, but calm. "Oh, yes, they'll make fun of you at first," she said. "You're a Colonial, you know."

"But," said Janet, enraged, "what if I am? I can't see I'm different."

"It's partly the way you speak," soothed Moira. "A sort of little sing-song. You'll get over it."

"I don't want to," Janet said. Her feeling of belonging here was going, rapidly. "I hate England. Beastly place."

"Don't talk like that," advised Moira, jumping down from the fence. "In a week or so you'll be loving it, simply *loving* it."

They went into the house together, and into their respective flats. Mother met Janet at the door, with a calm, pleased smile.

"What do you think, Jan? We've got a maid! She came this morning and I really think she's going to be satisfactory. Her name is Mrs. Murphy."

On top of *that*, one couldn't moan about girls following one home from school. Mother was so cheerful about the maid, and Janet, who had developed a protective feeling for her, couldn't spoil her happiness. She knew how hard it was to get a good cook.

"That's wonderful, Mother," she managed to say.

"Dinner's ready, ma'am," said Mrs. Murphy, padding heavily into the room. She was very stout and Irish. When she walked the floors shook, so did her chins.

They sat down at the table and Mrs. Murphy billowed in again, bearing proudly a beef-steak-and-kidney pudding of such quality that Janet's spirits began to rise. Strange how food always helped one to feel better!

Mother served the pudding and smiled across the table.

"Now," she said. "What about school? Did you like it a lot? Tell me all about it—don't miss a single thing."

The next week was a difficult one. The two girls still followed Janet part way home, and she still continued to be unhappy about it. She didn't say anything at home, because Mother was having troubles of her own, troubles with Mrs. Murphy.

"I don't know what to do," Mother confided. "She's a wonderful cook and she has a nice disposition. But I think she's a little queer in the head. I hear her talking to herself in the kitchen, and when I go in she's looking up the chimney in the *strangest* way. Little men live there, she says, little green men. Sometimes they talk to her and sometimes they help her, but most of the time they play tricks on her. What do you think we should do about it?"

Janet considered. It made her feel very grown-up when Mother talked to her like that; very grown-up and very close to Mother.

"Well," she said, "perhaps she's a bit dotty, and perhaps she's just Irish. And she *is* a good cook. Why don't we let her stay, unless it gets worse?"

So Mrs. Murphy stayed and cooked delectably for them. The little men didn't get seriously in the way, except that if anything was burned they provided the finest kind of alibi.

"Sure it was the little men," Mrs. Murphy would say, regarding overcrisp bacon sorrowfully. "They took me attention from it." And there was nothing one could say to that.

The Laidlaws put up with that, as they put up with Bombay Duck. Somewhere in her cooking experience Mrs. Murphy had learned to make a distressing pudding, consisting mainly of fried bread with jam on it, which she called, inaccurately, Bombay Duck. It was her favorite, if not the family's. The little men liked it too, they insisted that she serve it at least once a week.

Meanwhile, if Mrs. Laidlaw was getting resigned to Mrs. Murphy's ways, Janet was not at all resigned to the after-school situation. She had, at last, to tell Biddy about it.

Biddy fired up at once. "The brats!" she said. "I'll walk home with you today and see what happens." Much smaller physically than Janet, she was like a tiny, protective hen offering to a frightened chicken the shelter of inadequate wings. Janet did not think it at all strange; she accepted the offer gratefully, though she was not at all sure what Biddy would be able to do.

But Biddy was able to do much. When the silly giggles began, she turned, every freckle etched in gold on a white face, and stood her ground.

"You little beasts!" she said. "Teasing a girl from the Colonies, just because she's a bit different."

The giggles kept on. Biddy's face grew whiter, her freckles clearer.

"It's people like you who make trouble," she went on. "If the Colonies should decide they didn't want to belong to us, I wouldn't be surprised. It's people like you that start things—that make things happen——"

It was very dramatic, not entirely unpremeditated, because she'd been planning the speech in her mind, planning it carefully. And because Biddy was one of the most popular girls in the form, the words had effect.

"We didn't mean anything," the red-haired girl mumbled.

"It was just fun. And when she minded it we kept on, and it was more fun."

"Fun!" Biddy's eyes snapped. "If that's your idea of *fun*, you're darned poor sports."

"It isn't really," the fair-haired girl spoke up quickly. "I don't know what made us do it. We won't do it any more."

"Better not," counselled Biddy. "You don't want to break up the British Empire, do you?" She was too carried away with her own eloquence to know how funny it sounded. Janet smiled a little, she couldn't help it. But the other two girls didn't smile, they fell behind, walking solemnly, without giggles, keeping their eyes on the small, ruffled person ahead of them.

Biddy walked all the way home with Janet, parted from her at the gate.

"I'll take the tram back," she said. "And, Janet, Mother wants you to come to tea on Saturday. You know where we live."

Chapter
10 THE KING
IS DEAD....

SCHOOL SETTLED DOWN to pleasant, everyday happenings. History and geography, algebra and French, English and physics, the innumerable subjects of an English secondary school. Hockey and netball and gym. Exciting inter-school matches with every one wearing the school colors.

And on Saturdays and holidays there was London, a fairy-tale in gray, a place where anything might happen. There was magic and enchantment in going to town for the Christmas pantomime, or looking with fascinated but frightened eyes at the Chamber of Horrors in Madame Tussaud's Waxworks. And Buckingham Palace with the Coldstream Guards in their scarlet uniforms! Once, as Janet and Moira stood there, the royal carriage came out and lovely, gracious Queen Alexandra seemed to bow and smile directly at them.

"Mother has a friend who is housekeeper at the Palace," Moira said importantly. "And she has asked us to tea next Saturday."

Janet sighed. "How scrumptious! How perfectly posh! Nothing like that ever happens to me. Bring me home a piece of cake?"

After the tea Moira did actually appear with six small frosted cakes. "These were left over from Their tea," she said with awe. She set the cakes out in a pink-and-white row on the table where they sat in proud beauty until Jean said: "But can't we eat them?" Wistfully, "They look so good."

"I suppose they have to be eaten sometime," Moira said sadly. "But it seems a shame."

When the last royal crumb had vanished, Janet and Moira felt very close to the Palace. Since Moira had seen the royal apartments, the King and Queen seemed almost a part of the family. So it was a special and personal sorrow when one day at prayers Miss Garner, looking out over the roomful of upturned faces, said: "Girls, this morning we have the news that the King is seriously ill." And, in solemn words:

We pray that Thou wilt watch over our beloved King, and, if it be Thy will, restore him to health. Bless the Queen and be with her in these anxious hours.

The girls were silent as they went back to their rooms. The silence and the heaviness grew as the days passed.

"He *can't* die," Moira said. "He *can't*!" She and Janet read the papers eagerly and shuddered when the black borders told, without words, of the death of the King. Spreading the paper on the floor, the girls read it from the first page to the last. The papers made the most of the occasion, and when the funeral came, they played on every string of human sympathy. The King lying in state; the sad Queen; the flag-draped coffin followed by the King's favorite horse, stirrups reversed; the King's bewildered little black-and-white terrier wandering forlornly through the Palace. The whole nation was in mourning, black in cars, in busses, on the streets. The girls at Wimbledon Hill wore black ties. There was no color anywhere.

Then came the slow climb back to normal emotion. The papers carried pictures of the new King and Queen and their family of golden-haired, blue-eyed children. There were many doubts. Would the King be strong and steady enough to take the place of his father? Familiar talk to those who had seen Victoria go and Edward come, but leaving the younger generation to feel, for a short period, like a ship without a pilot.

After a decent time of mourning, London dressed herself in her best to welcome the new King and Queen. Janet and Moira went up to see the preparations for the Coronation. They walked across Westminster Bridge where rows of bright banners held the coats-of-arms of the Empire. "There's India!" said Moira. Janet said, "I suppose Trinidad isn't big enough to be represented." They were both thrilled by the pennants on which the scarlet Scottish lion clawed fiercely at his yellow background. On they went, trying to recognize old friends in the gaudy disguise that they had taken on. Buildings that had been there since early days peered, a little self-consciously, through their draperies of bunting. Red-white-and-blue, red-white-and-blue, the pattern was repeated a thousand times. Through Birdcage Walk, up Constitution Hill, on feet that were beginning to tire, to Hyde Park where they found a bench on which to rest.

"I'm worn out trying to see everything," Moira said.

"Look," said Janet. "You can't let down, even here!" For the carriages that were rolling past them were drawn by the most high-stepping of horses. And on the doors of the carriages were the coats-of-arms of all the royal houses of Europe.

On the night before the Coronation, the night of the Illumination, Janet went with Moira and her mother to see London put on a still more brilliant, jewelled dress. Lights—and lights—and more lights. Along the Strand, along the Mall, strings and strings of lights. Crowds and crowds and crowds; gay crowds with a holiday spirit, growing a little impatient when they became so closely packed as to make any sort of forward movement impossible.

"God save the King!" shouted an enthusiastic man in evening clothes, staggering a little.

"Gawd sive the King, me eye," a Cockney voice from the crowd. "Gawd sive *me,* hi sye. Where d'you think you're goin' anywye, mister?"

The crowd pushed its way up the Mall, that broad way that leads to the very gates of Buckingham Palace. Pushing, struggling, trying to go both ways at once. "Look out there for the byby . . ." "Hi sye, missis, why'd you bring a pram in all this? . . ." "Let a guy get 'is breath, won't yer? . . ."

Janet found herself pushing and struggling with the best.

The crowd leaned on her so heavily that the breath seemed all squeezed out of her. She was going to be crushed to death, she was sure of it. And to be crushed to death and miss the Coronation would be a tragedy. With a fierce determination to stay alive, she pushed a fat woman off her chest. The fat woman protested. "Tyke it easy, dearie. I ain't got no plice to go."

The crowds swayed and pushed and complained. And at last some of them fought their way to the open space before the Palace, and Janet was with them. They stood there packed in a solid mass, their faces turned expectantly upward. The solemn gray building looked back at them; the statue of the Queen Victoria looked down with all the primness of her time. Nothing happened. A few small boys climbed boldly on the railings. A sentry glared at them. "Get arf the rylings of ryalty," snarled the fat woman, who was, herself, practically one with the railings.

Murmurs ran through the crowd. "Ain't they comin' out? Ain't they goin' to give us a sight of them?"

Then on a balcony in the center of the palace there appeared a man and a woman, who stood there looking out over the crowd.

"'Ere they are, Gawd bless 'em!" And although the people were so tightly packed that it was almost impossible to get the breath to sing, the words rolled out, full and clear:

> God save our gracious King,
> Long live our noble King,
> God save the King.
> Send him victorious,
> Happy and glorious . . .

The King and Queen bowed acknowledgment. The crowd cheered itself hoarse, cheered again and was off on the strange, militant stanzas of *Rule, Britannia*:

"Britons never, NEVER, NEVER shall be slaves!"

On the mounting crescendo of defiance the King and Queen withdrew. The crowd began to mill about, to find its way out of the space into which it had jammed itself. Janet, when she could get a little breath, sighed: "It was wonderful! Though I think I'm black and blue all over."

But the next day they were all sufficiently recovered to see the Coronation procession. For long hours they sat on hard benches waiting for the procession to come. Jean shifted and sighed, kicking her heels restlessly.

"I don't want to wait so long," she said.

"But it will be worth waiting for," Moira assured her. "And it won't be long, now."

"I want a bun," said Jean. "And lemonade."

"Look," said Moira. "It's coming!" A ripple went through the crowd. "It's coming!"

And what a procession it was! Soldiers of every regiment, English, Scottish and Colonial—the Dominions and the Colonies sending their best from every corner of the world.

"There are the Sikhs!" Moira leaned forward in excitement as a fierce-looking Indian regiment went by.

"And the Aussies! The Canadians! And there's the Black Watch!" Scotland's famous regiment swung past to the shrill music of bagpipes.

Now the gilded coach with its eight horses was coming in

sight. All whispering stopped. The crowd rose to its feet with a great roar. Thousands of flags waved wildly. There came the peculiarly long-drawn-out British cheer, "Hip, hip, hoo*ray*! Hip, hip, hoo*ray*!" in waves of sound advancing with the royal coach. "Long live the King!" "Long live the Queen!"

They sat in the golden coach bowing to right and left. The King was a quiet man who seemed to feel the weight of the crown. Queen Mary with her golden hair and blue eyes was a queen every minute, smiling without fatigue at her people.

The coach went by, the shouting died down Jean, her eyes shining, slipped her hand into Janet's. "Did you see?" she whispered. "Did you *see*? They had real crowns—like in fairy tales!"

The pageant was over. Britain had taken the new King and had given him the same firm place as the old. All over the country fat red pillar-boxes that up to this time had held the proud E. R. that stood for *Edvardus Rex* changed to G. R. Stamps bore the picture of George the Fifth. Letters went on being posted. Life went back to normal.

Chapter
11
THE SILVER PENCIL

ALL THIS TIME the silver pencil had been lying idle, tucked into a corner of Janet's writing case. She was too busy at school to think of writing stories. It was the chance turning of pages in a magazine that brought the pencil out of its hiding place.

The magazine was *The Throne and Country,* an aristocratic sporting periodical that, for some reason or another, ran a children's page. The editor of this page, who wrote over the somewhat peculiar signature of Felix Noël, offered prizes for the best stories written by children under sixteen. Janet read the stories over thoughtfully. She could write as well as that, she was sure. And perhaps the silver pencil would bring her luck.

It didn't at first. The stories came winging home with disgusting speed. Janet was almost discouraged, but she kept on writing. And, quite suddenly, one day the silver pencil, almost of its own accord, swung into a story called *The Mantle of Night*. It was the kind of story that almost every young person who likes to write produces at one time or another. But it had its own distinction and a certain originality of plot. It dealt with a country in which the sun and moon were equally bright and the people had no sleep until a magic web, woven by millions of spiders, was thrown by an eagle, who flew up for that purpose, over the moon. Then her light was softened, and, when she drew the mantle more closely around her, there was night. When a corner of the mantle blew aside, it was moonlight.

Felix Noël's letter was enthusiastic. Janet had won first prize for the month. "An unusual story." But it was the prize that counted. When it came, Janet didn't open it at once; she waited until Moira and Jean could come in. They came at a gallop, for they knew about *Throne and Country* prizes and they weren't going to miss anything.

First the brown wrapping paper, then tissue paper tied with silver cord. Mrs. Laidlaw joined the gallery of onlookers, and even Mrs. Murphy came out of the kitchen to see what was going on. Though, she said, she had already known what was going to happen; the wee men in the chimney had whispered it in her ear.

Now the tissue paper was being folded back and the box appeared in all its glory. Shining white, with a proud *Fuller's* in silver script across the cover. Fuller's chocolates! No English child could wish for more.

The cover lifted, the chocolates stood in close brown ranks, a pair of silver tongs lying invitingly on top. It was a five-pound box, too heavy to pass around, so every one leaned over to take a chocolate with the silver tongs.

"Praise be to God," said Mrs. Murphy, as she took hers, "and to all the saints. Sure, I'll be making Bombay Duck for dinner, being as it's a special occasion." She shuffled back to the kitchen and to her conversations with the wee men.

Now, fired by success, the silver pencil went into a perfect burst of story-writing. There was a story about a king's messenger in scarlet, changed, for his misdeeds, into a scarlet runner vine. A story about how daisies came to close their petals at night, as is the way of small, pink-tipped English daisies. Twice more during the year the postman brought that wonderful package. And then came a heavy blow—a letter from Felix Noël.

"You have won three prizes," he (or was it she?) wrote. "And, as next month you will be sixteen, you will no longer be able to compete. Perhaps it is just as well for our other readers. Good-bye, and good luck to your stories."

Janet felt as if the bottom had dropped out of everything. The silver pencil would have been tucked away again if an idea, that seemed a perfect inspiration, had not come to her. Moira wasn't going to be sixteen! She hadn't won three prizes —in fact, although she'd sent in stories, she'd won no prizes whatever. Her stories were of a different type, heavily, painstakingly of this world, written without a touch of anything to lift them above the ordinary.

Janet could hardly wait to get over to the Somervilles' flat. She found Moira on the hearthrug, placing a row of chestnuts on the grate. "Moira, you know that story of yours about the boat on the beach? The one the children painted blue? The story you're planning to send to *Throne and Country*?" Janet hoped she was keeping some of the eagerness out of her voice.

Moira's thoughts were occupied with chestnuts. "That chap's almost roasted. Oh, yes, that story. I don't think I'll send it in. I never get a prize, anyway. Have a chestnut?" She picked a fine brown one off the grate with the tongs and set it on the hearth. "Let it get cooler, though."

"Thanks," Janet said absently. "But Moira, *we* could win a prize! I mean, if we wrote the story together. And sent it in under your name."

Moira brightened. "Right, o!" she said. "Let's start."

So when the chestnuts were roasted, the thin little story was spread out on the dining room table and Janet began to "do things" to it. The ordinary blue-painted boat became a magic one in which the children sailed to faraway lands. There were seaweed fairies—shrimps and lobsters that talked. The story's own mother didn't recognize it when Janet had finished with it.

Moira read it over. "It doesn't sound much like me," she said. "But Felix Noël likes that sort of thing. Let's try it, anyway."

The story was carefully put into an envelope and addressed, stamped and posted in the pillar-box on the corner. And in due time came a package for Moira, and a congratulatory letter from Felix Noël. It was not until the copy of the *Throne and*

Country arrived with *The Blue Boat* in print that Mrs. Somerville realized what had happened.

"Moira," she said as she finished reading the story, "this doesn't sound in the least as if you'd written it. Are you sure that you did?"

"Janet helped me," admitted Moira, looking up from the game of Ludo that she and Janet and Jean were playing.

"Do you think that was fair?"

"I—I don't know."

The whole transaction began to take on a different aspect. Up to now the girls actually had not thought whether it was fair or not. Neither of them would have dreamed of cheating at school, neither of them had thought that this was practically the same thing.

"I only meant to make a *few* changes," said Janet unhappily. "But when I started to write——"

"You simply re-wrote the whole story." Mrs. Somerville was sympathetic but firm. "What are you going to do about it?"

"We've eaten the chocolates," Moira sighed.

"In that case the only thing to do is to let it go. I don't believe it would do any good to write to Felix Noël."

"Oh, *no*," from both girls. "*Please!*"

"Then, *no more writing together*. Moira can try her own stories, stand on her own feet."

But Moira didn't. The gates of *Throne and Country* swung shut and there were no more boxes of Fuller's chocolates. Surprisingly enough, Janet found that it wasn't the absence of chocolates she minded, it was loss of the outlet for her stories. Now there seemed to be no reason for writing. The silver pencil lay quietly on her desk.

Chapter
12 *PICNIC IN THE RAIN*

IT WAS the morning before the closing day of school. Janet had awakened to a cold damp drizzle, had closed her eyes again and snuggled down under the bedclothes.

Then she remembered. The Lower Fifth was having its picnic. They were going to that darling little wood just beyond the Common. This was no morning to stay in bed. But what a day!

By the time the Lower Fifth had assembled, the rain had become more than a drizzle. The girls crowded around Miss Edwards in their macs and rain hats. Their faces were worried. Suppose they couldn't go! Think of all that heavenly food going to waste. Of course they could eat sandwiches in the gym, but what was the fun of that?

"Do you suppose Teddy will let us go?" The question passed from one girl to another.

"Miss Edwards—are we going?"

The form mistress looked down from her desk at the eager faces. Never very strong, taking cold easily, she yearned for a nice warm dry morning in the gym. But she couldn't disappoint them. They were such fine girls—it had been a good year.

So she said, with an enthusiasm she didn't feel, "Of course we're going. Every one got a mac?"

They plodded up the hill to the Common, a wide stretch of heath made bright by the yellow of gorse and broom, the purple of heather. It was two miles, but they didn't mind that.

Rain dripped from their hats, they pulled the collars of their macs closer to keep the drops from trickling down their necks.

Across the heath, the gorse glowing from the rain, the purple of the heather brightened by it. At last they came to the wood —a small wood that in the early spring had been yellow with primroses. Under a tree they sat, with the raindrops finding a way through the branches, splashing on their faces. Only in England would they have picnicked in such weather. It seemed to them, however, not to be out of the ordinary—if one waited for the weather nothing ever happened.

The sandwiches were unwrapped. They didn't seem to taste any the worse for being a bit damp. Janet found herself sitting next to Miss Edwards, offered her a ham sandwich.

Miss Edwards accepted the limp bread, bit into it cautiously, looked thoughtfully at Janet.

"Janet," she said. "Did Miss Garner tell you that you were getting a double remove?"

Janet's heart turned over. "No, am I?" She tried to sound unconcerned. "How ripping! She didn't tell me that—just told me I had made a record, with no disorder marks." She had made up her mind to try for this, the whole form had helped. Monitors looked the other way, articles in the Lost and Found box were never claimed, because claiming them meant disorder marks.

Miss Edwards smiled a trifle grimly. "Don't pat yourself on the back about it! We all know the story of *that* cooperative effort! But I'm glad about the remove. You'll be in the Sixth next year."

Janet couldn't think of anything to say. The sixth form! Next year! It couldn't be possible.

Miss Edwards went on: "And Miss Garner says that with a little more attention to algebra you should be able to win a scholarship for Girton. You'd like to, wouldn't you?"

Like to! Miracle of understatement. Girton was the girls' college at Cambridge. To think that there was a chance!

"I'll work like a dog at algebra," Janet said. "Will you have another sandwich?"

They went on with the picnic in a leisurely manner, the rain splashing a little harder through the trees. Then, the remains gathered up, they started back across the heath.

All the way home a great happiness walked with Janet. There was a clear happiness even in the gray drizzle of the day, in the familiar sights and sounds of the street, in the swing of the empty picnic-box in her hand. Happiness went with her into the flat, filled the living room as she entered, was in her voice when she spoke.

"Mother! Isn't it wonderful! Miss Garner says I can have a double remove! Next year I'll be in the sixth form. And Mother, Teddy says if I work hard I'll be sure to get a scholarship for Girton."

She put the picnic-box down on the table, threw her hat in a chair, unbuttoned her mac. Then, for the first time, she noticed that her mother wasn't smiling, wasn't sharing her joy.

"Why, Mother! *You aren't glad*."

"Sit down," Mrs. Laidlaw said in a tight voice. "We'd better talk things over. I wasn't going to tell you today, but now I think I'll have to. You can't go to Girton, Jan, in fact you won't be in school after the summer. We are going back to Trinidad."

Janet could not say a word. She sat there looking at her mother as if she were a strange person.

72

Mrs. Laidlaw went on, quickly, nervously: "There are lots of reasons. I know it's hard for you—but when we talk it over, you'll see how it is."

Will I? Janet wondered. She still couldn't speak, so she listened.

"I have a feeling that it won't be too long before Lawrence marries. It's probably our last chance to be with him, and to be back, for a while, in the House on the Hill. And I'm dreadfully homesick for it, aren't you?"

"No," Janet said. "And I don't want to leave school at sixteen. I want to go to college. I want it more than anything in the world."

"As for that," Mother said, "we couldn't afford it. Not even with a scholarship. We've had a hard time as it is. The scholarship would pay only your tuition, there would be all the college expenses—and clothes."

Janet looked at her mother. They had grown so close in these last years, Mother had really seemed to understand how she felt about things. But now it was as if a long, long road stretched out before her, a road she did not want to travel. And far in the distance, so small she could scarcely see the expression on her face, was Mother, beckoning to her to come.

"Well?" said Mrs. Laidlaw. "I had to tell you."

Janet brought herself back to reality with an effort. "I suppose so," she said dully. "But somehow I wish you'd waited until tomorrow. I was so happy—and now it's all gone."

"I did what I thought was best," Mrs. Laidlaw said. Her eyes filled with tears.

Then the floodgates opened. Janet went into her room and cried. She cried all that afternoon until her eyes were so swollen

73

that she could scarcely see out of them. At tea time she came out, ate miserably amid the sympathetic clucks of Mrs. Murphy, went back to her room, and cried again. It was only from sheer exhaustion that she stopped.

And when she was able to listen again, her mother went on:

"I didn't tell you the whole truth about our going to Trinidad, because I didn't want to worry you, but I'll have to tell you if you're going to take it like that. The doctor says I can't stand another of these English winters—I've got to go to a warm climate."

That helped. In solicitude over her mother's health, Janet almost forgot her longing for college. Almost, but not quite.

There was, now, only the one more day at school. Speech day, with the girls in their white dresses, and an air of eager anticipation. In the Lower Fifth, the girls crowded around Teddy's desk. They would have liked to say what a wonderful year it had been, but they had no words. No teacher in the school was better loved, and last days came hard.

"Janet," said Miss Edwards, "something tells me you are head of the form. That Girton scholarship isn't going to be difficult."

Janet, near to Miss Edwards' desk, looked up at her miserably, tried to say something, couldn't. Miss Edwards glanced at her sharply. A girl didn't usually look like that when she was head of the form.

The bell rang. The long line of girls went out into the hall, down the steps. Janet had a feeling that this was her first day at school. But it wasn't, it was her last.

They were in the assembly hall now, long rows of white-clad

girls. Miss Garner came forward, raised her hand, the girls dropped to their knees.

. . . *Almighty God, Who has safely brought us to the beginning of this day, defend us in the same*——

The voices rose and fell. Something in Janet's throat choked her so that she could not join in. The very familiarity of it—the dear familiarity.

The girls were on their feet again. Today they did not sing the school hymn. Their voices were clear and fresh:

> *Land of hope and glory,*
> *Mother of the free,*
> *How shall we adore thee*
> *Who are born of thee?* . . .

That was England! Suddenly there came over Janet a feeling of all that England stood for. She couldn't have put it into words, it had simply become a part of her. England was green fields . . . white cliffs and sandy beaches . . . woods yellow with primroses or blue with hyacinths in the spring . . . waiting at the gates of the Palace for a glimpse of the King and Queen . . . the ivy-covered buildings of Wimbledon Hill . . . England was far more than that. It was years of history, years of tradition, the building up of a way of living . . . the way of a people . . . her people . . .

The song was over. The girls had filed one by one up onto the platform to get their reports. Janet *was* head of her form—but now it did not matter in the least. The exercises were over, it was time to go home.

Moira was waiting at the gate. Janet and Biddy walked out of school together, but Biddy was going in the other direction.

She looks awfully white, thought Biddy. I wonder what's the matter?

They were at the gate. Biddy shifted her school bag slightly on her shoulder.

" 'Bye!" she said. " 'Bye, Jan. Good hols! See you in September."

" 'Bye," said Janet. "Thanks. Thanks a lot, Biddy."

She stood there by the gate, watching until Biddy turned the corner and was out of sight. Then, with one long backward look at the school, she fell into step beside Moira.

Chapter
13 *THE HEATHER HILLS*

THE GLOOM was relieved by the bright outdoor days of summer and the fact that Mrs. Somerville was going to take Janet and Moira to Scotland. Mrs. Laidlaw didn't want to travel that far, and, anyway, she had a fearfully English feeling about Scotland. She and Father had gone there after they were married and the visit had not been a shining success. "In the first place I didn't know the language," she said. "And in the second place I don't like porridge." She was very final about it.

But Janet longed to go. Brought up on the porridge that her father had believed essential to the growth of a Scot, understanding the Scottish tongue because he had read it aloud to her, she could not leave England without seeing her other country. The Somervilles had relatives in Edinburgh; that was where they would stay, and Janet would visit her uncle in Selkirk.

"I'm going to Selkirk with you," said Moira. "Because I've never been on a sheep farm and it must be frightfully exciting."

So, on a day that was unusual for Scotland, a bright, clear day with scarcely a cloud in the sky, the two girls took the train that went from Edinburgh to Selkirk. There Janet's uncle was to meet them and drive them to the farm.

The train sped peacefully along, but there was nothing peaceful in Janet's feelings. Here was the land in which her father had grown up. The heather hills—she was going to see them for herself! Now they were out in the open country, traveling between fields with the stone walls and gray cottages that made Scotland seem so different from England. Then—how the change came about, the girls did not know—suddenly the world was purple. On every side, like purple velvet, rolled the low hills. They had not known it would be just like that.

Janet's uncle met them at the train. With him were a girl and boy of about Janet's age and Moira's. That he was her uncle, Janet realized at once; he was so much like her father. Rather shyly, because he made no move, Janet spoke first.

"I think you must be my Uncle George?"

"Aye."

"And this is my cousin Sheila?"

"Aye."

"And Jock?"

"Aye."

"This is my friend Moira Somerville."

"Aye." (They shook hands with her solemnly.)

Was it going on like that forever? The silence was unbroken as they climbed into the wagon in which they were to drive to the farm. It finally grew so heavy and oppressive that Janet felt something must be done about it. She tried again.

"It's a beautiful day, Uncle George."

"Aye, it's that."

"And the heather is so pretty."

"Aye, it's braw."

Three words weren't much of an advance over one. Janet felt about in her mind, unsuccessfully, for topics of conversation. The next remark was contributed, surprisingly enough, by Jock. It was quite without context.

"Sheila found a saxpence oot forbye the dyke, Setterday," he said, hurrying the words together so that they sounded like a foreign language. Janet found herself translating them mentally. "Sheila found a sixpence by the stone wall, Saturday," and saying politely, "Oh, did you, Sheila?" She was glad that they were nearing the farmhouse as no one seemed to be able to think of anything more to say. But there was the house, a sturdy one of plain gray stone, built for winter protection in a bowl of low hills. On the sloping hillsides were stone sheep-pens, and, scattered here and there, white dots that were grazing sheep.

Aunt Annie met them at the door. "Weel, here ye are and I'm glad to see ye. Did ye have a guid journey? Ye'll hae had a fine chat wi' ye're Uncle George, I'm thinkin'. Aye but ye're a bonny, big lass. And is this the wee friend ye wrote of? Come in and bide by the fire a bit—it's cauld the day."

The words flowed on and on, but it was a relief to find some one who could talk. By tea time Aunt Annie had not run down. Janet and Moira were exhausted by their efforts to listen and translate.

Tea was magnificent. It was "high tea" with cold chicken and ham as well as the scones and jam and cake. Janet and

Moira stuffed themselves to the ears. And toward the end of the meal, Moira's over-burdened interior gave a long, low, protesting rumble. Aunt Annie, pricking her ears in the direction of the barnyard, held up a finger. "Jock, wasna that the coo'?"

"Na," Jock said. "It wasna the coo'." His brown eyes met Moira's, full of merriment. She decided that she liked Jock in spite of his tongue-tied awkwardness. Shaking back her curls, she bit firmly into another scone for which she had absolutely no room.

"And noo' we'll be drivin' over tae see yere Aunt Gracie," announced Aunt Annie. It sounded simple, but it wasn't. At Aunt Gracie's house there was a gathering of the clan. Not a real clan, for they were Lowland, but all the relatives within walking or driving distance. It was a time of true Scottish hospitality. And there was another tea, with more scones and buns and fruit cake.

"Do you suppose there comes a time when one really and truly *bursts*?" Janet whispered to Moira.

"I don't know," whispered Moira. "I think I'm getting a sort of second wind."

"The lassies hae nae appetite," mourned Aunt Gracie. "Will ye no have a scone?"

When they were all as full as boa-constrictors and almost as torpid, Aunt Gracie suggested a visit to the churchyard, so that Janet might see the graves of her ancestors.

"I don't think I want to see them," Janet whispered to Moira.

"But you *have* to," Moira whispered back.

Jock came over to them, then. "It's no sae bad in the kirkyard," he said reassuringly. "It's braw up yon the hill."

It *was* beautiful. The stark little church stood amid trees on a high knoll looking out over the purple countryside. Janet was pleasantly thrilled by the tombstones which bore the names of departed relatives—and after each male name, FARMER or SHEPHERD. There was a solidity about those words that pleased her, even though she knew that one of them represented the family skeleton; her grandmother having eloped with one of her father's shepherds.

"It was up here in the kirkyard that your grand-uncle, William Laidlaw, wrote *Lucy's Flittin'*," said Aunt Gracie, whose speech was less broad because she had been to boarding school in Edinburgh. "He and Wattie Scott and James Hogg were having a chat up here when they saw a puir orphan girl leaving the home she'd been working in. So your Uncle William and James Hogg—who was a bit poet—made up a wee rhyme about her."

"I don't know *Lucy's Flittin'*," Janet said politely.

"Then ye should, for it's a good auld Scottish poem. Did your father never say it to you, lassie? Ye must read it."

"I will," said Janet. If her Uncle William could write, perhaps she could, too. Not poems, she had never tried one since that first effort. But stories, better ones than she had written for the magazine, perhaps—some day a book. Oh, she would like to write a book! She would like it better than anything in the world!

They went back, after that, to the farm. Aunt Annie and Sheila went indoors; the others stayed out for a while.

"Dinna gae in yet, lassies," said Uncle George. "Ye'll be wanting tae see the sheep brought in."

In the gray mist of the evening there was a quiet peace. Now the sheepfolds on the hills were in shadow; twilight had deepened the purple of the heather. Janet knew, suddenly, why her father had chosen, so often, to read the twenty-third psalm at family prayers. She seemed to hear his voice as they sat around the lamp-lit table in the House on the Hill:

The Lord is my shepherd; I shall not want.

He maketh me to lie down in green pastures: he leadeth me
beside the still waters . . .

and her own voice taking up the words as the big Bible passed from one to another; stumbling over them a little when she was *very* young:

Surely goodness and mercy shall follow me all the days of
my life:

And I will dwell in the house of the Lord for ever.

She came back to reality with a start as one of the sheep dogs came up and put its cold, wet nose in her hand. Janet patted the dog's shaggy head.

"He's wanting tae gae," Jock said. "Bide a wee, Robbie, it's no time yet."

"I'll gie them the signal." Uncle George snapped his fingers. "Robbie, Colin, Mac, here lads!" The dogs gathered eagerly around him, intelligent eyes alight with anticipation, plumy tails wagging.

"Off wi' ye, then! Bring them in!"

The dogs were off with joyous barks. Guided only by soft whistles from Jock, they rounded up the sheep, drove them into the pens. Thoroughly competent sheep-herders, they never made a false move.

"They're wonderful," Janet said.

"Aye," said Jock, his brown eyes shining. "They are guid dogs. Robbie's mine. He had second at the sheep-dog trials this year. Next year I'm thinking he'll be first."

Now it was almost dark and the air was growing colder. The shepherds were coming in, their day's work over. Janet had a glimpse of them sitting around the big fireplace in the kitchen as she and Moira went into the house. Father had told her how Sir Walter Scott came often to sit with the shepherds in the farmhouse kitchen.

In the parlor, Janet and Moira scrunched themselves over a peat fire. There was a deep chill in the air. Aunt Annie's voice still flowed on like a restless brook. At last she seemed to run out of talk and the girls gave small sighs of relief. But, gathering her forces once more, Aunt Annie turned briskly to Jock. "Play us a wee tune on yere fiddle," she said.

Jock rose awkwardly and reached for his violin. Sheila went to the piano to accompany him. It was going to be perfectly terrible . . .

And then Jock, his violin tucked under his chin, moved the bow slowly and lovingly across the strings. And, after the tuning, the music came, strong and clear, rising above Sheila's wholly inadequate accompaniment, finally taking the room to itself so that Sheila need not have been playing at all. The old Scottish songs, the wailing lament of *Flowers o' the Forest*, the gay lilt of *Wi' a Hundred Pipers an' A' an' A'*. Then quite spontaneously, as the tune changed, they were singing with him:

> *Bonnie Charlie's now awa'*
> *Safely o'er the friendly main.*
> *Mony a heart will break in twa*
> *Should he no come back again.*
> *Will ye no come back again?*
> *Will ye no come back again?*
> *Better lo'ed ye canna be.*
> *Will ye no come back again?*

The music ended on the pleading refrain, and Jock put the violin carefully into its case. He came over and sat by Moira. The fire burned low. And nobody, not even Aunt Annie, said a word.

Chapter
14 HOUSE ON THE HILL

In LATE September, when Biddy and Moira and all the others were back at Wimbledon Hill, Janet and her mother went back to Trinidad. Lawrence met them with his temperamental but shiny new car. The forty-mile drive through country villages and sugar estates was like a dream. Janet had a vague feeling of having lived here before, but no real sense of familiarity. The streets of San Fernando, which had once seemed so broad, were small and narrow. The first true feeling of homecoming began when they passed the market, still red-roofed, still alive with color and still giving out the most extraordinary smells. Mrs. Laidlaw did not have her smelling-salts now, nor did she seem to feel the lack of them. But she said, "I should think the town would do something towards cleaning up that dreadful market."

"We are planning to move it to another part of town and build a library here," Lawrence assured her.

Move the market! Janet could not bear the thought. But her mother felt that a library at the foot of the driveway would be far more elegant, and she thoroughly approved the plan.

"I hope it will be a handsome building," she said. "After all, we have to look down on it all day long."

"It should be," said Lawrence. "It's a Carnegie library. We are very proud of getting it."

Janet was doubtful that even a Carnegie library would make up for the loss of the market, but she said nothing. They were coming to the bend in the driveway. The old cocoa tree still carried its pods of pink and maroon; the bamboos were green and feathery as before. They turned the corner, and there was the house, looking no different. After all, they had been away only four years.

Janet had a queer feeling that the snake would be weaving on the step, but instead a very small black-and-white dog came down to meet them. Wagging her whole body, curling back her lip over her teeth, snorting in greeting, she put her tiny paws up on Janet's dress.

"That's Beatrice," Lawrence explained. "Bea for short. She's a one-man dog, but she'll take you in somewhere on the fringe."

"And there's Pussy!" Pussy, showing none of the infirmities of age, stood on the top step, waving his tail. When that vulgar little dog had got through with her smiling and snorting, he would greet the family. But Janet did not give him a chance to be dignified. Running up the steps, she gathered him up and hugged him.

"Pussy! How glad I am to see you!"

There was no change of expression on the tough old face, but Pussy purred and kneaded her with his paws.

Lawrence, helping Mother out of the car, looked up at them and laughed. "I think that cat's going to live forever. Why, he must be seventeen years old! And just as cross and independent as he always has been."

Mother came up the steps, briskly for her, stopped and looked around the dark-panelled drawing room.

"It looks much the same . . . *what are those on the ceiling?*"

Janet and Lawrence looked up. The ceiling was entirely covered with huge moths, their metallic blue wings outspread.

"They—they weren't here yesterday," said Lawrence. "Must have moved in last night. Rachel!"

Rachel, thin and yellow as ever, came into the room, shook hands with Mother and Janet. "Yes, Mr. Lawrence?"

"Do you know anything about these moths?"

"No, Mr. Lawrence. This morning they was here. That's all I know."

"Can't you get them out? With a broom or something?"

"No, *sir!* Not me. When *Mortbleus* come in a house they stays till they wants to go. Ain't good luck to send them out."

"Oh, well," said Mother amiably, "I suppose we can stand them. But I hope they move on soon." Her eyes roamed over the room. "Lawrence! *Those pictures!*"

Lawrence looked at the pictures uncomfortably. He had been running the house as a bachelor establishment, with two of his friends, and lovely ladies, lightly clad, had replaced *The Blue Boy, The Laughing Cavalier,* and *Lovers' Quarrel.*

"The boys wanted them," he said lamely. His eyes, so much like Father's, met Janet's and a look of understanding passed between them. It grew into greater understanding later in the day, when they restored Mother's choice of pictures and took the lovely ladies out to the stable-garage. Janet leaned the pictures gently up against the wall. "Poor dears. It will be a dull life for you." Then she had an inspiration.

"Mother never comes out here. Let's hang them up!" Lawrence got hammer and nails, and the ladies were hung on the stable wall, where they clutched their scanty draperies and smiled vaguely down at their reflections in the shiny car.

"I don't see what you two find to laugh about when you are out in the stable," puzzled Mrs. Laidlaw.

"You'd be surprised," said Lawrence. "Stables can be awfully amusing places." Janet's warning glance said, "Don't say too much, or she'll go out there."

"Only *you* wouldn't see anything funny," he added hastily.

Mrs. Laidlaw sighed. "I suppose not. You two are so much like your father. Half the time I didn't know what he was laughing at."

"That was the trouble with her. She didn't," said Lawrence, as Mother went to the pantry to give directions to Rachel, now the housemaid. "Were you old enough when Father died to realize what a wonderful sense of humor he had?"

"I certainly was," Janet said. "I can see the way his eyes crinkled up when he laughed. Do you remember the time we were having family prayers and MacGregor came sneaking around and Father laughed out in the middle of the Bible reading?"

"Mother never got over that!" Lawrence chuckled.

"She's a dear," Janet said, "but she certainly doesn't see the funny side of things."

"She isn't going to see the funny side of my parrot," said Lawrence. "You haven't met him yet. Probably he's out in the mango tree. Come on, let's see if we can find him."

They walked across the yard. Janet looked up at her brother. She had rather dreaded meeting him again, he was so much older than she, but now she knew they were going to be friends. Under the mango tree they stopped and Lawrence whistled.

"*Caramba!*" said a hoarse voice, and a green parrot peered down at them from the branches.

"You see!" said Lawrence. "I got him from a South American sailor, and he has a red-hot collection of swear words."

"Mother doesn't know Spanish, so she won't know unless you tell her."

The parrot sidled along the branch, cocked its head and said in tones dripping with sweetness, "Love me, dearie? Kiss?" and made loud kissing sounds.

Janet laughed. "I'd know he'd been living with you and the boys."

"And that isn't the worst he can do." Lawrence was gloomy. "We had too good a time teaching him—well—things."

"*Bai la patte!*" said the parrot in patois. "*Bai la patte!*"

"No, I won't shake your hand," said Janet. "Not until I know you better. And go easy on the things you say to Mother—at least at first."

"*Caramba!*" screeched the parrot, scrambling up to another branch. "Polly's a bad, bad bird."

Janet and Lawrence walked back to the house, stopping on the way to look at the new tennis court which had displaced the croquet lawn.

"Can you play?" asked Lawrence.

Janet nodded. "Didn't I live in Wimbledon? Wimbledon lives and breathes tennis."

"Good," he said. "I asked one of the fellows to come up to-morrow afternoon and he's bringing a girl with him. Her name is Mary, Mary Shoreham. She's a Canadian girl who's just come down with her father, who's a bank inspector. You might like her."

"Why? Why do you think I'll like this girl?"

"I don't know. I've only met her once, but I think you'll get along. I hope you brought your racquet?"

They were back at the house now, and as they went up the steps there was a dull, whirring sound. Without any special reason except that it seemed to be time for them to go—the *Mortbleus* moved on together like a shining cloud.

Chapter
15
A MATTER
OF SLEEVES

JANET AND Mary were playing singles. "What's the score?" Janet asked. "I'm getting awfully hot, aren't you?"

"Hot! That isn't the word for it. I can't see why any one ever thought tennis was a game for the tropics. The score is thirty-forty in your favor."

"Let's finish this set and get cooled off. We're pretty evenly matched but your serve is swifter."

When the set was over—Mary had won—the two girls sat on the grass under the big saman tree by the side of the tennis court. Blossoms like small pink powder-puffs dropped into their laps.

"You sit down so quickly," Janet said. "I can tell you haven't been here very long. I always look carefully to see what I might be going to sit on. Ants, for instance."

"Ouch!" said Mary. "I forgot. Well, I didn't sit on anything, but I leaned back against the tree and something is crawling down my spine. Take a look, will you?"

"You're awfully calm about it," said Janet. "But then you are

88

calm about everything." She peered down Mary's back. "Whatever it was, it isn't there any longer."

They settled back against the tree to talk. "I'm glad you came," Janet said. "Since I went to England I've rather lost touch with my old crowd. It's lucky we get on so well."

Mary nodded. "That happens when you go away. And I'd be dreadfully lonely without you. . . . Good heavens, is that a dog?"

"It's Bea. Not looking her best, because she's going to have puppies. And she always laughs like that. I think she's a weird little thing, but Lawrence is devoted to her. He always takes her in the car—as you'll find out when you go driving with us. She sits on the hood and breathes down your neck. And she's likely to have her pups in the car."

"That will be perfectly *lovely*," said Mary. "It's crawling again."

"What, the ant?"

"It's not an ant. It's something much, much larger. It's coming down my arm!" Mary shook her sleeve violently. "Janet. It's a lizard!"

"So it is." Janet looked without emotion at the tiny creature on the grass. "Rather a pretty one. No, Bea, don't touch it."

"But it was down my back! It crawled all over me."

"Yes, I know. I had one down my back, once. Bigger than this one."

"Well," said Mary. "Maybe the first hundred years *is* the worst. I can't quite get used to things. I can't even get used to seeing East Indians all over the place. It doesn't seem natural in the West Indies."

"They were brought here to work on the sugar estates," Janet said. "By the way, Mrs. Fraser at the East Indian Mission has asked me to write a play for some of the little girls. She wants me to coach them, too. Want to help?"

"I'll do what I can," Mary said. "But I think I'm better at tennis. Still, it should be fun. Anything we do together is apt to be."

"I've started the play. It's Japanese. No reason except that the costumes are pretty and the children can do nice things with fans. We'll start rehearsals next week."

Perhaps a Japanese play was not the best choice for six little East Indian girls, but they took to it like ducks to water. They chattered about their dresses and sashes and the chrysanthemums that they would wear in their hair. From home they produced cheerfully un-Japanese fans with pink ladies on them—fans that had been given away by a local store at Christmas time.

"Be sure to keep them picture side out, so the printing on the back doesn't show," advised Janet. "Myrtle, speak more slowly. Phoebe Lahori, speak up, we can't hear a word you say. Louise, don't stand on one foot. Carol, try not to giggle."

"They are darlings," Mary said. "But my pet is that older girl who plays the mother. Lydia, you call her, don't you?"

"Yes," said Janet. "But there's something strange about her. I never feel she's really here with us, some part of her is always far away. Her eyes don't see us."

"Anyway, she's beautiful," Mary said. "I used to teach girls of her age. Maybe I can find out what is the matter."

"Try it. I'm better with the younger ones."

But Mary, sympathetic though her approach was, got nowhere with Lydia. The day of the dress rehearsal came with Lydia still going through her part mechanically; adequate, but aloof. The girls were lovely in their Japanese costumes, and in spite of Lydia, the dress rehearsal went well.

"But, Lydia," Janet pleaded, "can't you show a little more feeling? Can't you cry when your little girl is hurt?"

"No," said Lydia briefly. She never wasted words.

The day of the play arrived. The hall was filled with relatives and friends full of eager anticipation. The children—all but Lydia—were in the dressing room when Janet and Mary got there. And one glance showed the girls that all was not well. In the first place, Lydia was not there. In the second place, the little girls had cut the flowing sleeves from their dresses, and there was an array of thin little brown arms.

"Children, what have you done to your sleeves?" Janet's voice was despairing. "And what is the matter with your faces?"

"We thought short sleeves had more style." It was Phoebe who explained. "And actresses always wear rouge."

"Not brown-skinned ones," Janet wanted to say, but caught the words back in time. The children were so happy, what did it matter after all? The most serious thing was not the sleeves or the grotesque little faces. *Where was Lydia?*

"I'll try to find her," Mary said. But at that minute Lydia came in. Her sleeves still flowed, her cheeks were unpainted, but her big dark eyes were swollen with crying. The audience was growing restless, there was nothing to do but start the play. And so the curtain went up.

It was a great success. And at the time when Lydia should have cried and never did, she dissolved in a perfect flood of tears. All the emotion that had been lacking at rehearsals was there. The audience stamped and clapped. But, the play over, Lydia did not stop to take her curtain calls. Tears still streaming, she rushed through the back door, and was across the yard to the Mission school where the older girls boarded. Mary went after her. It was a long time before she came back, and when she came there were tears in her eyes.

"Did you find out—" Janet almost hesitated to ask. In the short time she had known Mary she had found out how difficult it was for her to talk about things that moved or distressed her. "Can you tell me now that the children have gone?"

"Yes," said Mary. Words came to her slowly, not easily, as to Janet. "I found out. Lydia is in trouble with her family. She's been having a romance. A harmless little one, but one that did not please her father and mother. She's been talking to the boy who sweeps the school yard every morning. Just talking. Nothing more than that. But she likes him, even if she is only twelve. And one day he gave her a present—an old pair of gold-rimmed eyeglasses—of all things—and her parents found out."

"They marry at that age—and younger—" Janet's voice was puzzled. "But what harm does it do for her to like the boy?"

"It's a matter of caste. She's high caste, he's low. And her parents have already promised her in marriage. Her mother came here this morning and raised an awful fuss. Made Lydia bow down to the ground seven times to show her submission. Now they're taking her home to their house and they say she can't come back to the school. She'll never see the boy again— and soon she'll be married to another boy she's never met."

"Poor kid," Janet said. "No wonder she cried. I feel so sorry for her. And there isn't a thing we can do about it."

"Not a thing." Mary's voice was rough with feeling.

Janet looked at her curiously. "Don't take it so hard. Better come home to dinner with me. Call your father up and tell him you're going to spend the night with us."

In Janet's room that night the two girls stood at the window looking up at the Hill. It was beautiful in the bright tropical moonlight. The bamboos wove a silver pattern against the sky and the light silvered the fronds of the coconut palms.

"Coconut trees are lovely in moonlight," Janet said. "And look at the saman tree. The whole world is lovely."

"For us, but not for Lydia," Mary said, the tightness still in her voice.

"But it helped for her to tell you about it. I'd never have got a thing out of her."

"Oh, well," Mary was casual. "I told you I'd taught girls of her age, and I seem to know how to get on with them. I thought you were grand with the younger children, Jan. I was glad you let them keep their funny pink cheeks. I wonder——"

"Wonder what?"

"Oh, nothing. Just something I was wondering about you. Some day perhaps I'll tell you. But not tonight."

Chapter
16 *THE GREAT DECISION*

THE NEXT DAY Beatrice had her puppies, four of them. She came into the house elegantly slim, pleased with herself, grinning and making those funny, snorting sounds that passed for laughter. The puppies, she showed them, were under the bridge at the entrance to the stable. She, Bea, had dug a little cave in the soft clay with her own paws—clever, wasn't she?

The puppies, to the first casual view, were like any other pups Bea had produced. Two of them were white with black spots;

rather surprisingly two of them were black. It was only after a couple of weeks that every one realized what large puppies they were, and how rapidly they were growing.

"Bea!" Lawrence said. "Don't tell me they're half *collie*. I can't stand it." Bea snorted with pleasure. She was proud of these giant pups of hers, but she wasn't going to feed them. She knew her limitations. Lick them and keep them clean, yes. Keep a maternal eye on them, yes. Feed them, no. So the pups had to be brought up on the bottle, and most of the time it was Janet who supervised the feeding. Bea sat and watched with interest and when the meal was over she came up to Janet wagging her tail and snorting with laughter.

"Only it isn't a joke," Janet assured her. "I don't enjoy coming down here at all hours to do the job you won't do."

One afternoon Mary had come with her to the stable for the four o'clock feeding. Janet sat on a pile of hay, the smallest black puppy in her lap. He sucked noisily at the bottle, his small tummy comfortably distended by the warm milk.

"I'm tired of it," Janet said suddenly.

"Of what?" asked Mary. "Feeding the pups?"

"That's only a part of it," Janet said. "I mean I'm tired of being here in this island with nothing to do but feed puppies and play tennis. You know how I wanted to go to college."

"I do know," Mary said. "You should have had the chance. But you want to write—those stories you showed me are *good*."

"Fair, but I won't write if I stay here. I know that. The tropics make you lazy—you lose ambition." Janet put the satisfied black puppy down on the floor, picked up one of the black-and-white ones. In his eagerness he almost knocked the bottle out of her hand. She gave him a little shake.

94

"Greedy thing! No wonder you're growing so fast. Why, you're almost as big as your mother. Easy there—you'll choke!"

"I don't think you should stay here and feed puppies," Mary said. "You have ability and you should use it. Why don't you go to Canada—or to America?"

The bottle almost slipped from Janet's hand. Canada? America? Mary might as well have said, "Why don't you go to the North Pole?" Canada. America. They sounded equally far away and unattainable.

"What would I do there?"

Mary considered. "You're fond of children. I told you I liked the way you worked with them when we had the entertainment. That was what I was wondering about the other night."

"And I'm fond of puppies. But that doesn't get me anywhere."

"Being fond of children does. You could be a kindergarten teacher. Why don't you take a course in kindergarten teaching?"

It was as simple as that. One minute the idea had not been there at all; the next it was not only there but seemed the most logical thing in the world.

"I'd love to do it," Janet said. Her voice shook with eagerness. "But what would Mother say?"

"Try her," Mary advised. "I've got to go home now, but why don't you talk it over with your mother?"

Janet walked very slowly towards the house. At this hour her mother was always sitting on the gallery. She was there now, and Janet noticed, with surprise, that she was wearing a white dress. Since Father died she had worn nothing but black. What had brought about the change? Was it a good omen?

As she went up the front steps and onto the gallery Janet saw the green parrot sidling up and down the railing. He had, much to the amusement of Lawrence, developed a passion for Mother, and she seemed to return his affection. He could even look at her with his wicked little red eyes and say "Kiss?" and she would smile indulgently.

"Mother," Janet said, sitting in the chair beside her, "I didn't know you had a white dress."

Her mother smiled. "I had it made. You know, I've discovered that Polly doesn't like black. He likes visitors who are dressed in white."

Janet tried not to laugh. "So that's it! Well, Lawrence and I are tired of black, too."

Mrs. Laidlaw looked at her sharply. "And you are tired of Trinidad. I've been noticing it, Jan."

The approach was wide open. Janet rushed into it. "Yes, I am. Of course I like the House on the Hill and I like being here with you and Lawrence. But there isn't enough to *do*. Mother—" her voice was urgent—"Do you think I could go to Canada—or America—to take kindergarten training? I think I would like to teach."

There was a deep, cool stillness. Mrs. Laidlaw looked out across the Gulf as if she had not heard the words. The parrot sidled furiously up and down, his eyes glowing red. *"Caramba!"* he exploded.

Janet laughed. "No, Polly, it's not as bad as that. Mother, aren't you going to say something? Please?"

"It's hard for me to say anything." Mrs. Laidlaw's voice had a faraway sound. "You are my only daughter, you know. But, looking at it fairly and squarely, I think you should go. You haven't really been happy since we left England. Yes, I think you should go."

Her mother's attitude was a great surprise to Janet. It was, after all, Lawrence who objected. There was no need, he said, for Janet to work. Girls didn't need to work—at least not in their family. America—Canada, they were too far away. She was too young to travel alone.

"I'm almost eighteen," Janet said. "And, anyway, I'm going to write to training schools for their catalogs."

When the catalogs came they were thrilling from cover to cover. Clark Training School in Brooklyn seemed to offer the best courses. That, Janet decided, was where she would take her training.

"If you *must* go," Lawrence came to it at last, "I'll write the Scotts to meet you and look after you." Alan Scott had been his partner for some years after Father died; now the Scotts were living in Brooklyn.

The weeks of preparation were rather like the weeks when they were getting ready to go to England.

"I wouldn't take too many clothes, if I were you," advised Mary. "They won't look right in America."

But Mrs. Laidlaw insisted that Janet be well supplied, that she order some clothes from England, have others made for her. And, as the time for leaving drew near, was only three days away, Janet suddenly realized all that she was leaving. The House on the Hill, her home, Mother, Lawrence—Mary, so recently become her friend.

"I can't go!" she said and cried from morning until night, the quiet continuous kind of crying that finally leaves one completely worn out.

"Oh, yes, you can," said Mary. "You're not going to back out at the last moment."

"I wish you were going, too!" Janet said to her mother.

"I wish I were. But this climate is better for me than a northern one. I'll stay with Lawrence, at least for a time."

The day came. Farewells were not tearful because all the tears had been cried in the days that came before. Lawrence was going to take Janet to the boat—Mrs. Laidlaw and Mary thought it would be better if they stayed in San Fernando. Bea laughed inappropriately when Janet told her good-bye. The puppies staggered over and licked her hand with their warm tongues. They were enormous now, all of them except the little black one, as big as Bea.

"Good-bye, Beatrice," said Janet. "Be good. And don't have any more puppies for a while. I won't be here to look after them." Bea snorted and wagged, but made no promises.

Part 3

AMERICA

$\mathcal{A}$MERICA

Chapter
17 ON THE THRESHOLD

THE TOWERING skyline of New York looked down on a boat that was being pushed slowly into a Brooklyn pier.

"Get in there!" puffed the small important tugs. "Get *in* there, *in* there, *in* there!" with impatient jets of steam.

Janet stood by the ship's rail, looking up at the tall buildings. Thousands of square window-eyes looked back at her, coldly. They don't like me, she thought. Suppose Americans don't like me? Suppose I don't like them? Suppose I can't be a teacher? She had a habit of thinking things like that, of crossing bridges before she came to them.

Well, however things might be, here she was and there was no turning back. Eight days ago she had been in her safe, comfortable home with her mother and Lawrence. Eight days ago she had said good-bye to it all. Now she was on the doorstep of America, not being very sure whether the door would open for her or not.

The tugs had finished their job and were puffing, with all the arrogance of small fry, out into the river. The hawsers had been made fast to the pier, the gangplank lowered. People were coming aboard, meeting their friends. The deck was full of laughter and greeting. So these were Americans! They didn't look so unlike the British. Janet smiled to herself at the absurdity of her thoughts. How had she supposed they would look? Like people from Mars?

She stood expectantly at the head of the gangplank, waiting for her friends to come. Alan Scott and his wife; she hadn't seen them for years, but she would know them at once. Funny how late they were!

The deck began to clear, the passengers were going off. Now only a few were left. These went, too, and Janet realized that she was the only passenger on the boat. Desperately she leaned over the rail to get a view of the pier. Not a familiar face!

The third officer came by, whistling. He was a nice boy with red hair; Janet had danced with him almost every evening.

"Hi, there, Trinidad! Like us too well to leave?"

"No," Janet said dismally. "There's no one to meet me."

"Wow!" His teasing changed to quick sympathy. "What a bad break! They won't let you go ashore. Better come down with me and talk to the immigration officers."

They went down to the dining saloon. The immigration officers were friendly but firm. No, she couldn't land. Of course not. If no one met her she would have to go to Ellis Island. They were sorry, but regulations were regulations.

Janet felt a little faint. "Oh, I'm sure they'll come," she said bravely. "My brother sent a cable. I'll go up and wait on deck." She turned and walked up the stairs.

Now the window-eyes looked at her more coldly than ever. She slid into a deck chair, a great wave of homesickness coming over her. Quick! She must think of something, anything but the fact that no one had come to meet her. All kinds of pictures drifted through her mind. She thought of all the events that had led up to this bold—or was it rash—step of hers; coming to America alone. These were the things that had made her the kind of person she was—the person America would like, would not like, who could teach, could not teach. The words went round and round in her head. The skyline melted into the sky —vanished. Now she was seeing only the friendly, familiar outlines of the House on the Hill.

"Hullo, Janet! Dreaming? Welcome to America!" The voice was Alan Scott's. He and Lillian were standing by her chair looking down at her. Janet brought herself sharply back to reality.

"We're so sorry," Lillian was saying. "Somehow Alan got the idea that the boat docked at four instead of at two. I hope the time hasn't seemed long."

"Oh, no," Janet lied politely. "Not *too* long." She had only lived through years in those two hours, but she certainly wasn't going to let them know.

"That's fine. We must go down and clear your papers. I hope the immigration officers are still here." Alan was offhand about it, and, after all, it was quite easy now that he had come. In half an hour they were ashore. "This," said Janet to herself, "is Brooklyn." Her ideas about Brooklyn had been hazy. It had seemed to be a sort of suburb of New York; she was surprised to find it a large and independent city, with endless streets of houses. The Scotts lived in a doll-like house a long way from the docks, in a street with many other doll-houses all exactly alike. The sidewalks were full of children and baby carriages —prams to Janet—of dogs and express wagons. The little girls wore big bows of ribbon on their hair, the boys looked like Buster Brown. It's all very much like the *Ladies' Home Journal*, Janet decided. And how funny it was that the houses had no fences! How did they know which lawn was whose?

The next day was even more strange and terrifying. Alan Scott took her on the "El" to Clark Training School. She had dressed herself carefully for the occasion in a long white knitted coat that had looked very fine when it came from England. On the train she realized that it was a unique garment, no one was wearing anything that looked remotely like it. She began to feel uncomfortable and out-of-place.

At the door of the kindergarten training school, Alan Scott left her. Now her legs must carry her up that flight of steps, and they weren't going to, she was sure of that. But somehow they did, and somehow she found herself sitting rigidly erect on a chair in Miss Beck's office. Miss Beck, a white-haired woman who looked like a small, fierce eagle, was the head of the training school. Janet knew, as the keen eyes travelled from her hat to her shoes, that her clothes were not right; definitely they were not right. She felt as if the eyes had peeled the unsuitable clothing off her, had left her nothing but her underwear—which was presumably suitable either for England or America. But Miss Beck, though crisp of manner, was cordial. After a brief talk with Janet, she called in a girl who happened to be passing the door.

"Helen Chapman! Will you take our British girl to the cloak-room and help her find a locker? Then both of you should go to music class."

Helen was a sturdy girl, not pretty, but with friendly eyes and a perfectly enchanting smile. Janet felt she was in good hands, wondered if Helen would like her, or merely think her "queer." Helen herself answered that as she shepherded Janet through the halls.

"I'm feeling every bit as new and strange as you are," she

confided. "I'm from New England, and I'm as homesick as anything. You see, I've never been away from home, not even for a day. Let's stick together!"

"Right, o," said Janet. It sounded frightfully British and not at all the thing to say, but Helen seemed not to notice. They were, by now, going into the classroom where many girls were grouped around a piano. Miss Warren, the music teacher, had been a professional singer, she played the piano as if in a concert hall. They would, she explained amid a series of crashing chords, begin by singing songs that were familiar to them all.

The songs were familiar even to Janet. Why, she had grown up on *Old Black Joe* and *Seeing Nellie Home*! She could sing with the rest.

Then the piano went into even more familiar music. Janet gave a little start. So Americans sang British songs? The chords crashed out, the girls began to sing:

> *Land of hope and glory,*
> *Mother of the free,*
> *How shall we adore thee*
> *Who are born of thee?*

In imagination Janet was back in England again, it was the last day at Wimbledon Hill. Then she noticed the girls' intent faces. They were singing the song as if it were their own. Why, they didn't know it was an English song . . . *They were singing it about America*! She would have to tell them it was English. No—that wouldn't do, she had better not say anything.

"Let's sing the *Battle Hymn of the Republic*," suggested one of the girls. The piano crashed into the music. Janet was puzzled. That—why *that* was *John Brown's Body*. She had grown up on it, too, in many strange and ribald variations. But these words were not the ones that she knew. These words were serious:

In the beauty of the lilies Christ was born across the sea,
With a glory in His bosom that transfigures you and me;
As He died to make men holy, let us die to make men free,
While God is marching on.

So they were singing it as a national song! A strange country, America. Glory hallelujah, *how* strange!

* * * *

As the days went on, Janet found the kindergarten curriculum also strange and full of surprises. Almost immediately, the girls made the acquaintance of Freidrich Froebel, that gentle, peculiar genius who was the founder of the kindergarten. In this particular training system he was the center of everything, all theory and practice revolving around the things he had written and done and said. He was so omnipresent that it made one a little uncomfortable. There were many tangible evidences of his teaching. The children in the kindergarten brought their small green chairs each morning and placed them on a circle painted on the floor, gathering together for "morning circle." They stood on the circle when they played games, for Froebel had been convinced that the circle gave a feeling of "unity." He had devised a series of playthings called "gifts." The first gift consisted of six rainbow-colored balls on strings—on her first day of teaching Janet would learn what pitfalls lay in this innocent plaything. It was all rather difficult. Froebel's children, easily regimented, had probably taken kindly to standing on a line, to playing in prescribed ways. American children were too experimental for a young teacher's peace of mind.

On the third day, the Junior Class went to play games in the gymnasium. Janet went eagerly with the rest, supposing they would play the old folk games she had always known. But she found that Froebel had built up a series of games with an "inner meaning." They were dramatic singing games in which one had to play a part. Janet and Helen stood watching as a group of girls played "The Birds' Nest." Some of the girls were baby birds, huddled together in an imaginary nest. Two were the father and mother birds and flew, with flapping wings, to find food for the little ones. They returned to the nest to spread protective wings over a group of what Janet should have seen as baby birds, but saw only as large girls making small ridiculous cheeping sounds.

"I *can't* play that!" she whispered to Helen. The next game was even worse. The girls impersonated knights who rode on prancing steeds in search of a good child.

"I know I can't do *that*," Janet whispered again. But her name and Helen's were being called for the next game. Horror of horrors—they were both chosen to be knights. Helen, not as self-conscious as her friend, didn't seem to mind it. What disturbed Janet the most was that she was going to have to *sing*, not as one of a large group, but as one of three. She shut her eyes and prayed silently, "Oh, Lord, help me to keep on key." Then the piano began the galloping music and they were off. Janet galloped feebly, tried to keep up with the others, felt herself growing beet-red.

"Pick up your feet," Helen whispered, breathlessly. "Prance!"

Janet made a noble effort and pranced fairly well. Now the tune changed and it was time to sing. Her throat grew dry, her tongue seemed to cling to the roof of her mouth. The other girls burst into song as they galloped down the long floor of the gym:

Three knights come riding this pleasant day
"Any good children here?" they say.

Janet opened her mouth, and not a sound came. But Helen's voice was sweet and clear, perhaps the gym teacher would not realize that one of the knights had been struck dumb. And at last the class was over, the agony postponed until another week. It was a mercy that Janet did not see what the gym teacher wrote opposite her name in the roll book: *Self-conscious. Doesn't sing. Must be developed. Give many chances to take leading parts.*

* * * *

The class in story-telling made up for the misery of games. Because Janet really loved stories, her shyness vanished. *Little Black Sambo?* Of course she could tell that. She knew just where the tiny book had stood on her bookshelf at home. It had been such a favorite that it had kept a warm little place of its own even when she was reading older books. She was moderately successful with that first story. The second assignment was a poem. The girls listened, fascinated, as Janet said it, hung with delight on the words of the last stanza as she rendered them:

> *By all these lovely tohkens,*
> *Septembah days are heah,*
> *With summah's best of weathah,*
> *And autumn's best of cheah."*

"Say it again!" they pleaded, following her out of class. "We love to listen to you." And, because they did not laugh at her,

Janet said it again. But, privately, she made up her mind to learn to say her r's. Helen couldn't help, for, being a New Englander, *her* r's were vague. In every other way she was a good friend. Janet couldn't have got through those first days without Helen's cheerful ways and friendly smile.

Chapter
18
FINDING A HOME

THERE WAS, now, the little matter of finding a place to live. The Scotts didn't have room to keep her—and anyway their house was too far from the school. The school secretary gave her a list of houses. "You may find that one of these will suit you." Her sympathetic and discerning eyes said, "You're a fussy one, I can tell it to look at you, and these *won't* suit."

Janet started out bravely, looked at small room after small room until her feet hurt and her head ached—her heart, too. The rooms all looked alike, one window, a bed, a dresser, a table; bare, unhomelike. "Of course, dearie," they told her, "you'll have your own couch cover and your curtains, it'll look more homelike." But it wouldn't. She could imagine the big shadowy rooms of the House on the Hill—the pink room had been hers when she went back. It was growing dusk now and she could see the maid moving softly in the room, pulling the mosquito netting over the big bed with its crisp linen sheets . . . but she wouldn't be pulling the mosquito netting, because there was no one to sleep in the bed.

She *couldn't* live in one of those cubby holes, she simply couldn't. Somehow she remembered that friends of her father's lived not too far from the school, Scottish friends. She'd go to them for advice. "May I use your telephone?" she asked the woman who owned variation number twenty of the barrack-like room.

"Why, we'd be delighted to see you!" Mrs. Monroe's voice was warm and friendly over the 'phone. Why don't you come up and have dinner with us? No, it won't make the least difference. Come along!"

The streetcar took her quickly to the Monroes' home. It was one in a row of comfortable houses looking all alike, two-family houses with a small garden in the rear, a railed porch in front.

The Monroes were all she had hoped for. Mr. Monroe was a little like Father, though his moustache was gray and his hair scant. His tongue had not lost the Scottish burr after years of living in America, not even though he had become an American. His wife, black-haired, blue-eyed, brisk and motherly, also had a trace of Scottish speech. The two sons, Tom and Stephen, two and four years older than Janet, were thoroughly American. Tom was the one who was especially nice to her; small, dark, she scarcely noticed him. It was tall, fair Stephen she saw —and who scarcely seemed to see her.

Mrs. Monroe's dinner was a wonder. And the grace was the one Janet had heard her father say so many times—"For what we are about to receive—" Just being in a family made her happily homesick. Rice pudding. With raisins. Mother made it like that.

Mrs. Monroe was saying, "So you couldn't find a place to live. What are you planning to do?"

"I don't know," Janet said. "I thought maybe you could help me to find a place."

Tom looked at her across the table, his keen dark eyes appraising her. "What about that extra room of ours, Mom? We don't often have a guest—"

Mrs. Monroe looked doubtful. "It's not a very big room—"

"Let her see it," suggested Tom—why did all the helpful suggestions come from him? Stephen, eating his dessert in placid fashion, seemed to be entirely uninterested in her affairs, interested only and intensively in rice pudding.

"Oh, do let me see it!" Janet said. She knew already that if the room were only the size of a postage stamp she would like it. For it wasn't a large room she wanted, it was any sort of a room with a home around it.

As soon as dinner was over they went to look at the room. It *was* small and there wasn't much in it but a bed, a dresser, a table and a chair. But there were frilly curtains at the window, a cheerful coverlet on the bed, bright rugs on the floor.

"It's perfect," said Janet. "Will you really take me in?"

"Indeed I will," said Mrs. Monroe. "And would you like to have your meals with us? Breakfast and dinner—you'll be away for lunch."

"I'd love it," Janet said. "You're awfully kind. May I bring my things here tomorrow? Or is that too soon?"

"The sooner the better," said Mr. Monroe in his hearty voice. "It will be like having a daughter in the house. The boys will be glad to have a girl around."

"You bet!" said Tom, clapping her on the shoulder. "More fun! You'll be here for dinner tomorrow."

Stephen turned, now, and looked her over, carefully. Janet felt acutely conscious of her lack of good looks. For Stephen was quite the handsomest creature she'd ever seen. And to think that she was going to be where she could look admiringly at him seven days of the week! He wouldn't look at her, of course, but what did *that* matter?

Living with the Monroes was the next best thing to living at home. To make things perfect, Helen lived with cousins of her father's only a few blocks away. They could go to school to-gether—work together some evenings.

At meal times she sat beside Tom, directly across the table from Stephen. She was glad it was so; she liked the way the light from the chandelier caught Stephen's hair and made it seem blonder than ever. She couldn't have seen that if she'd been sitting beside him. And he talked to her across the table, smiled at her.

The boys were as individual, as different from each other as any two brothers could be. Tom, serious and quiet, was finish-ing a business course. Stephen was in college, taking pre-medical work. His room was a clutter of bottles with creatures preserved in alcohol, the despair of his neat-minded mother. And his most precious possession startled Janet as she went past the door of his room. It was a skeleton that hung there, looking eerily out into the hall through eyeless sockets.

"Stephen," Janet said. "Why do you keep that terrible crea-ture in your room?"

"Terrible creature?" Stephen was puzzled. "Oh, you mean *George*. He isn't terrible and he's a great help to me in my work. In fact he's by way of being my mascot. I think I'll keep him in my office when I have one." He ran his hand affectionately over George's drafty ribs. George clattered a little.

Janet shivered. "Just hang him in your reception room and you won't have any patients. Wherever did you get him?"

Stephen chuckled. "He belonged to a doctor friend of Dad's. When he gave him to me I had a time getting him home. Had quite a brush with a cop. It's a long story but I'll tell it to you sometime."

That was promising. Perhaps Stephen would take her out some day and tell her George's story. Janet began to have a sort of affection for George, to fancy she saw an approving gleam in his vacant eyes.

But, after all, it was Tom who asked her to go out with him, to go to New York one evening to see Broadway, the lights of the city, to go to a movie. It was fun to go, of course, but why was he the one to ask her?

Broadway was a glittering river of lights; it was wonderful and something to write home about, even if she was seeing it for the first time with the wrong person. The movie was good. Afterwards, when they were in a drugstore and she was sipping cautiously at a chocolate soda—she wasn't quite used to sodas yet, nor sure she liked them—Tom talked more than he had all evening.

"You're a good kid," he said. "I'm glad you've come to live with us. But I'd like to warn you."

Warn me? thought Janet. Of what?

Tom went on: "It's Stephen. You think he's marvellous. All the girls do. Pretty soon he'll begin to notice you—and you'll fall for him—crash! bang!—the way they all do. Like a ton of bricks."

"I will *not*," Janet said indignantly.

"But you will. It never fails. And you're such a nice kid, I hate to see you let down. *Don't let him play with you.* He's never serious."

"I can take care of myself, thank you," Janet said. The dignity of her remark was spoiled a little by the fact that she had reached the bottom of her soda and the straw gave out empty, gurgling sounds.

"I'm not so sure," said Tom.

They walked out into the cool, glittering night, to the subway, home in silence. At the door, Tom turned to her again.

"Don't be so up-stage," he said. "Some day you'll be glad I warned you. You'll be *thanking* me."

"Good night. Thank you for a nice evening," Janet said, her voice more frosty than the night.

A week later when Stephen took her to the theater, she laughed softly to herself at Tom's dismal warning. Stephen was friendly, big-brotherly, but nothing more than that. In the darkness of the theater he didn't even hold her hand. That, she felt, was the least he could have done, she was disappointed. But of course Stephen wasn't the least bit interested in her, and why should he pretend to be? Tom must be jealous. It was strange, because Tom wasn't interested in her, either. He had a girl. Janet simply couldn't figure it out. It didn't worry her long, however, for soon she was lost in the play. It was *The Passing of the Third Floor Back,* with Forbes-Robertson. He was a very famous actor; Janet felt a thrill of pride in the fact that he was British. Watching a play like that, one forgot things small and personal.

Chapter
19
IN FROEBEL'S GARDEN

"Tomorrow," Janet said, "I start teaching." Pride was in her voice. It was to be her first day of practice teaching.

"Wait until you see the little Wops," said Stephen. "Sewed into their clothes for the winter."

"They aren't Wops and anyway I don't call Italians Wops and they are Scandinavian," Janet said a little incoherently.

"Well, wait until you see 'em and smell 'em." He grinned at her. They were good friends, now.

But Janet refused to have the picture of her first teaching ruined. She went into her room and got out her white shirtwaist and skirt, just to make sure they were spotlessly clean. The regulations for practice teaching called for three white outfits a week. The whiteness of the garments started a train of thought.

"White—angel—heavenly." Filled with sentiment, Janet sat down and began to write. The story grew quickly under her pen. It was a delicate little tale of a white-robed angel who tended a garden of beautiful flowers. Kindergarten—children's garden—heavenly garden, the train of thought was easy to follow. When the story was finished, Janet read it over with satisfaction. She would show it to Stephen. No, she couldn't do that, he would laugh. She might send it to Mother, but Mother might not understand. Mary? Oh, that was it! She would send it to Mary who would think the symbolism beautiful. So she folded the story, put it in an envelope and addressed it to Mary.

It was really too bad that Froebel couldn't have seen it, he would have enjoyed it.

Then she went to take a bath, for tomorrow she must be clean throughout, and there might not be time in the morning. No high priestess preparing for a sacred rite ever felt more sanctified. The sacred moment was spoiled somewhat by Tom's voice on the other side of the bathroom door.

"Hi! Aren't you ever coming out? Four other people waiting for baths. Shake it up!"

But such things were only on the fringe of consciousness, they didn't really matter. The sanctified mood held until after breakfast the following morning. Then cold, stark fright took its place. Janet tried to reason with herself. Why, there was nothing to be afraid of. She was going to teach sweet little children, and behind her stood Froebel with his superior wisdom. Of course there was nothing to be afraid of.

But fear was still with her as she transferred from one trolley at an intersection and stood waiting for the second car that would take her to the kindergarten. Willow Place—it had a lovely sound. The trolley was long in coming, the December wind was icy, and her coat did not seem as warm as it had been in November. Janet's teeth chattered.

When the car came, it was crowded, and the general atmosphere was warm, steamy and unwashed. Janet clung to a strap and remembered Stephen's words. "'Sewed into their clothes for the winter." Of course the children at Willow Place could not be like that.

The streets were dirtier now and they seemed full of children. The buildings were sordid, and there were bedclothes airing in the windows.

"Willow Place!" called the conductor.

Janet let go of the strap and found that her knees were strangely inadequate to hold her up. Somehow she got out of the car and walked down the short half block to Willow Place Kindergarten. She wondered, as she walked, why it was called Willow Place. All she could see was one scrubby plane tree.

The kindergarten was on the second floor and Janet shared the stairs with small children who stared at her unblinkingly. There was the same unwashed odor that she had encountered in the streetcar, but that, of course, was their winter coats.

At the head of the stairs a small hallway held racks for the children's wraps. The little creatures disposed of them with miraculous swiftness and ran for the kindergarten room. Janet followed more slowly.

Standing in the doorway she saw a large bright room with flowers in the windows, and a circle of small green chairs, in which some twenty children were already seated. They looked fairly clean and Janet felt a sense of relief. As she stood there, uncertainly, a plump, smiling woman with pink cheeks and white hair billowed towards her.

"Miss Laidlaw! Here you are! Come in and sit down. We are almost ready for Morning Circle. And I'll introduce you to the children."

Janet felt slightly ill. The geraniums and the chairs danced before her eyes in a dizzy pattern of red and green.

"But Miss Douglas, I don't have to have a group of my own the first day, do I?" (Always be positive in your attitude, Miss Beck had said, and here she was starting off with a strong negative.)

Miss Douglas looked slightly shocked. "Of course you do, my

dear! There's nothing like taking responsibility from the very first, and Miss Beck's girls are *always* equal to responsibilities. And emergencies."

"Ye-s, Miss Douglas." Janet gulped a little, then walked over and took a chair in the circle. On each side of her was a small, solid child, unmistakably flaxen and Scandinavian. They stared at her with cold, china-blue eyes. Other children were dark and obviously Italian.

The circle of chairs was filling up. Miss Douglas went to the piano and struck a chord. Fifty small children leapt to their feet and stood by their chairs like so many little statues. Miss Beck's words sounded in Janet's ears. "I have a feeling that your difficulty may be discipline. I am sending you to Willow Place because Miss Douglas is an excellent disciplinarian."

"We will sing our morning hymn," said Miss Douglas in the sweetest of tones. She played softly on the piano and one small boy bellowed out a raucous and individual, "GOOD MORNING!"

The little girls on each side of him scowled. Miss Douglas smiled patiently. "No, no, dear, wait until we all start." The small boy shrank into himself and his mouth remained obstinately closed as fifty small untuneful voices started:

> *Good morning to you, glorious sun,*
> *You bring the morning light.*

The sun streamed in the windows and touched some of the small golden heads. The cold feeling was leaving Janet's stomach, the sanctified feeling was coming back.

Morning Circle went on, with talk about the weather and baby sisters and brothers. The children were unbelievably good.

Janet's children, who proved to be the youngest, and who were both Italian and Norwegian, were introduced to her, holding out pudgy baby hands of varying cleanliness, staring at her with solemn baby eyes.

Then suddenly Morning Circle was over and ten quiet, demure babies followed Janet into a smaller room.

"We like to keep the babies by themselves," purred Miss Douglas. She handed Janet a basket of colored balls. "You will take the First Gift with them today. But perhaps you had better tell them a story first, a story always helps to create a friendly feeling."

So Janet found herself on a small green chair, with ten children on the floor beside her. It was vaguely unreal, and in the far-off distance she heard her own voice saying:

"Once upon a time there was a little black boy and his name was Little Black Sambo——"

Stories, unfortunately, last a brief time and soon the ten children and Janet were seated around the small table, with the basket of bright-colored balls in the center. Janet passed one to each child. They sat, balls held by strings, eyes riveted on her.

"Let's swing our balls," said Janet brightly.

> *Swing high—swing low,*
> *Swing to and fro.*

Eleven balls swung in perfect rhythm. It was all so charming and so easy. Then small dark Tony decided that Angelina's red ball was preferable to his own.

"Wanna *red* ball," he said, and clutched.

The red ball slipped from its owner's hand and rolled under the table. Like a flash Tony was after it and so were the nine others. The children and balls were in a struggling mass on the floor. Little girls began to cry. The uproar was terrible. Janet jumped to her feet.

"Children! Come out *at* once. Tony! Olaf! Angelina!"

But her voice was lost in the storm. The noise swelled and grew. Balls of all colors rolled on the floor. Legs and arms became a frightful tangle. Tony bit Angelina, her anguished wail could be heard above the din. Then, pink, unruffled, Miss Douglas appeared in the doorway.

"CHILDREN!"

The uproar stopped as suddenly as it had begun. Ten children were miraculously in ten seats. They were sitting round the table as demurely as before, but Angelina's ball was blue and Tony's was red. Angelina cast deep looks of hate at Tony, and caressed the tooth marks in her wrist.

"A little firmer with them, please," murmured Miss Douglas, and withdrew. After that things were fairly well. Janet did not attempt to make Tony return the ball, but a firmer tone came into her voice. Balls swung and rolled and went up and down to little tunes, then they were all neatly in their basket. Except Tony's and that remained clutched in his hand.

"Put it in the basket, Tony."

"BAsket, BAsket," Tony mocked her broad English A's.

"Let's have another story," Janet said hastily. That, she felt, was safe. There was something very satisfying about having the children on the floor, at a safe distance from the balls. She began the story.

"Once upon a time there were three bears———"

It worked like a charm. Her English intonations didn't seem to matter when she told a story. But, just as the baby bear found Goldilocks asleep in his bed, Janet looked up to see a frozen expression on Angelina's small dark face. And all around Angelina a puddle was spreading on the floor.

"Miss Douglas!" There was panic in Janet's voice as she went into the big room. "Angelina has had an accident——"

"Send the other children in here," said Miss Douglas, "and attend to Angelina. Miss Beck's girls——"

Janet didn't wait to hear the end of the sentence. She found herself wondering what Froebel would have done in such a case, and, surprisingly, she laughed.

"I'll take care of her, Miss Douglas."

With that laugh came freedom. Angelina's wails ceased and she laughed, too. And when Angelina was standing back to the radiator on which a small, grayish pair of panties was drying, Janet looked down at her with maternal satisfaction. Even if her discipline was not all that was to be desired, she had this day met an emergency and had conquered it.

Chapter
20 *INTERLUDE WITH STEPHEN*

IN THE SPRING the Junior Class gave *Cinderella* as a play. Janet, who was to be one of the pages to the King, designed the pages' costumes. They looked wonderful on paper—all white and silver, with silver lions rampant on cloak and tunic. But to make her own costume was another thing. For she could sew very little—she'd never been interested in it.

So on an evening when the rest of the family had gone out, and Stephen was working in his room, Janet brought the white material out into the dining room and spread it on the big table. Carefully she pinned on the paper pattern, cut around it. Well—it looked something like a tunic. Now to get it together. Perhaps she'd better cut the silver lions and paste those on.

That accomplished, she stood back and looked at the tunic. Now for the seams! As she threaded her needle a great light came upon her. *She did not need to sew.* Why not glue the seams together as she had glued the silver lions? The glue seemed remarkably efficient, it would probably hold through the dress rehearsal and the play. She took the brush and dipped it in the glue.

Then Stephen's door opened and he came out. He stood there for a moment looking at the picture that Janet made. The lamplight shone down on her hair, bringing out the gold lights in it. Her cheeks were pink with effort, her forehead wrinkled in a slight frown. At that moment she came as near to being pretty as she ever would. Feeling Stephen's eyes on her she looked up and smiled.

"Oh, Stephen, I hoped you wouldn't see this."

"For the love of Mike, what are you doing?" He came closer, looked down at the white tunic with its lions. "You funny kid— I believe you're *glueing* it together."

"Yes," Janet said in a small voice. "I—you see I don't like to sew." She waited for the shout of laughter, but it didn't come. Stephen took a step forward, put his arms around her, drew her back against him.

"You're sweet," he said.

Janet hoped he wouldn't feel her heart beating. It seemed to be behaving in the strangest way; to be quite beyond her control.

"You're very sweet," he said again, and kissed her on the lips. Then, his arm still around her, he turned her so that they faced the mirror over the mantel. They stood there for a minute, his cheek on her hair.

Far off in the distance, very faintly, Janet seemed to hear Tom's voice. "Don't let him play with you. He's never serious." It was very far off and it didn't matter in the least. What mattered was that Stephen was saying, looking not at her but at the girl in the mirror, "How do we go together?"

"We go very well," Janet said breathlessly.

There was the sound of a key in the front door. Stephen gave her a quick kiss. When Tom came up the stairs they were both standing by the table, and Janet had dipped the brush in the glue.

"Hi, there!" said Tom.

"Look what she's doing, the little nitwit," Stephen said. "Glueing her costume together. What d'you know about that?"

"Not much," snapped Tom. He looked them both over carefully. Janet felt her cheeks growing pink. Her secret, she felt sure, was written on her face. Hastily gathering up the partly glued costume, she went to her room. She couldn't have Tom looking at her like that, she wanted to be by herself, to think things over, to realize what had happened. She threw the costume on the bed, sat down beside it, looking into space, seeing nothing. Stephen loved her! Perhaps they were engaged. Perhaps—she didn't know. In her experience there had been kisses lightly given—lightly taken—but somehow this was different. It must mean more. Of one thing she was sure. She loved Stephen.

*　　*　　*　　*　　*

It was two whole days before they had a chance to be together again. Both of them were working, both came home just before dinner, and the house always seemed full to overflowing with family. Family in the dining room, in the living room, on the porch and in the kitchen—Janet had never known how full of family a house could be.

Then, on Sunday afternoon, they went to Coney Island. It was still cold and the boardwalk was deserted except for a few couples, all absorbed in each other. The sea was gray, the sky was gray, a few late flakes of snow began to fall. Janet shivered.

"Cold?" asked Stephen. Strange how much could go into one word! He smiled down at her, pulled her arm through his, closed his fingers warmly over hers.

"That's better, isn't it?"

Now it was a beautiful day, the sun was shining—it wasn't, of course, but it felt as if it were—and Stephen's hand held hers, closer and closer. He said nothing at all, but that was unimportant. Words weren't necessary. That was how it went— short moments of happiness—little said, apparently little need to say anything. Janet had an uneasy feeling that in books there always came a time when the hero said in plain words, "I love you," and passed on from there to "Will you marry me?" or its equivalent. Perhaps with Stephen there was no need for this. Sometimes in the mornings they were the first up, and Stephen gave her a hasty kiss. Why it had to be furtive and hasty she didn't know—she would have told the family—the world. But evidently Stephen wasn't ready to tell either the family or the world, so she would wait. It was rather nice, after all, to have it their secret.

Mornings, she felt, were quite a test of affection. If Stephen could stand the sight of braided hair and she could stand the sight of unshaven chin, everything was well. She did wish, occasionally, that he would get a bathrobe slightly more becoming to him than the somewhat ragged white Terry cloth that he wore. He should have cared that she was seeing him in an unattractive light. Perhaps this was the ideal way to approach marriage, to see the worst of each other beforehand. But had he said anything about marriage? Possibly in America that was the way, one wasn't formal about it. Yes, that must be the American way. And, having decided this, she was content. So content that she actually managed to come down to earth enough to finish the costume. She had misgivings about the seams, but they appeared to be strong. Suppose in the middle of the play they should all give way at once and the costume slide gently to the ground? She dreamed of it at night, dreamed that she was standing holding the pillow with Cinderella's slipper and wearing exactly nothing at all. It was an exhausting and chilly dream. She was glad that there were only a few nights before the play.

As a matter of fact, she need not have worried. The glue *was* efficient and the costume held. The worst that happened was that, at the crucial moment, a silver lion slowly detached itself from her cloak, curling with the heat, and fell at Cinderella's feet. Cinderella, however, had just put on the slipper and was looking up into the Prince's eyes, the audience was looking at Cinderella—and nobody noticed a mere page or a lost lion. Helen, who was also a page, picked up the lion, grinned and handed it to Janet a moment after the curtain went down. "Your luck was with you," she said. "Maybe if you'd learn to sew it would be easier on your nerves!"

Chapter
21
NEW ENGLAND

AT THE END of the school year, Helen asked Janet to go home with her. Home was a small town in Massachusetts. To go to New England! It had a far-off, remote sound, as if one should take a long sea voyage to get there. And it would be far—very far—away from Stephen. At first Janet thought she couldn't go. Then she remembered that separation was supposed to help if you wanted to find out whether you were in love with a person. She was sure of herself, but not of Stephen. Perhaps if she went away. . . .

So she went to New England. Apparently Stephen didn't mind very much. All he said was, "Good-bye, angel-face! Have a grand time and send me a post card." It could scarcely be considered romantic.

Janet had only the vaguest idea of what New England would be like. As the train went through the Connecticut countryside she was pleasantly surprised. It looked, she thought, very much like England. The fields, crisscrossed by stone walls, the cattle grazing peacefully by quick-running streams, the apple orchards, the winding roads. The sloping, stony hillsides were different—sterner.

"What rocky pastures!" she said to Helen. "The cows look as if some one had cut them out and pasted them on the hillside. I can't see why they don't fall off!"

"New England cows are smart!" Helen said. "They've grown up with rocks and hills. Do you know how all these rocks came to be here?"

"No," Janet said. "I can't imagine."

"It was because the Connecticut farmers made the Devil, who lived on Long Island, angry. So he took all the rocks that were on Long Island and hurled them over into the Connecticut meadows. And there they are to this day, making trouble for the farmers."

Janet laughed. But she was thinking to herself, "So there are old stories—legends—about this country, too. I thought it was too new for that."

When they came to Helen's home town she knew that New England wasn't so new after all. Perhaps it had been growing for only three hundred years or so, but the little town looked as though it had been there for a long, long time. The white church with its slender steeple, the solid white houses clustered around the village green, like prim old ladies gathered for a bit of gossip, the gardens with hollyhocks and delphinium, marigolds and petunias all had a satisfying feeling of permanence.

Helen's father met them at the station, kissed them both. "Your mother is at home," he said to Helen. "Said she had a pie in the oven and couldn't leave it."

And Helen's house! That was something to compare with the picture-book houses of England. Low and white, with shuttered windows and a dignified white door with a fine fan skylight. A seat each side of the doorway seemed to say, "Sit here and rest, and when you are rested we are ready to welcome you." Somehow, up to this time, Janet had thought of America in terms of apartments and two-family houses rather than as a country of gracious homes.

The white door opened and Helen's mother stood there, plump, motherly, smiling. Nothing restrained about the greeting of this mother and daughter. "Helen! Is it really you!" And Helen hugging her mother—making up for all the homesick months, yet almost instantly remembering Janet and drawing her into the warmth of her mother's embrace—into the house and into the family circle.

For, the moment she stepped over the doorsill of that friendly house Janet felt at home. Helen's freckled-faced young brother, and her small equally freckled sister were full of good nature. It was one of those families that are close knit, happy, taking strangers into the home so easily that in an hour they are no longer strangers.

The summer did its best, too, with long golden days and warm starlit nights. Plain days and special days. Dances in the big shadowy barn. Picnics by the river. Gay crowds of young people.

Janet loved it all. She was part of it; no one mentioned the fact that she was not American or asked her how she felt about America. Not, at least, until that August afternoon when they were all sitting in the garden, a little quiet, a little stunned by the newspaper headline of the day—ENGLAND DECLARES WAR ON GERMANY. Mrs. Marshall, who had been reading the paper, put it down, turned to Janet and said: "Tell us—how do you really feel about America? Frankly, I mean; we're not expecting you to think us perfect. Helen said you hadn't quite made up your mind about a number of things. And, with today's news, your heart must be very much with your own country. How do we compare with it?"

"Well," said Janet, after a little hesitation, "there are many things that I like about America."

"And other things you dislike."

"Not *dislike*. They puzzle me—make me feel sometimes that I don't belong here. The girls, for instance. They have so much assurance, they seem so much more independent than English girls of the same age. They grow up sooner. Sometimes I think they are *too* sure of themselves."

"But," said Mrs. Marshall, "did you ever think that when English girls were leading sheltered Victorian lives, American girls were bringing up their families in the wilderness—shooting Indians if necessary—going the long, hard way to the West in covered wagons? Might not that have made some of the difference?"

"Perhaps," Janet said. "I hadn't thought of it that way."

"And——"

"And one of the things I love about America is its friendliness. The way you took me into the family from the very first day, made me feel so much one of you. In England I went to visit some of my school friends, but getting to know their families took longer."

"That may be living in the wilderness, too," Helen said. "We grew to be friendly when there was danger everywhere. John Jones didn't walk primly up his neighbor's pathway and say, 'Pardon me, sir, but there are some Indians coming this way.' He dashed up the path, hammered on the door and yelled, 'Injuns comin'!' Informal, you see!"

Janet laughed. "Maybe so. I'm finding out a lot about America. But I'm still puzzled. People are *too* cordial sometimes. They promise things and don't do them. 'Call me up'—but they don't really care. 'Drop in and see me'—but it doesn't mean a thing. I've had some rather discouraging experiences along that line. At first I took everything at its face value. Then I learned that didn't work."

Mrs. Marshall sighed. "I'm afraid that *is* a weakness that goes with our warm-heartedness. You have to take them together. Sometimes our quick sympathies carry us away, and we promise more than we can fulfill. But that's on the surface. In a real emergency I think you'll find you can rely on us." She smiled. "We're getting very serious, aren't we? Tomorrow we're going to take you to visit an American family—one of the best."

Janet wondered why they didn't tell her the name. Why didn't they say, as they usually did, "We are going to see the Grays—the Bradshaws—the Starrs"? Why not?

They drove quite a distance the next day, through villages with their white-steepled churches, their square white houses, their spreading elms and quiet village greens. They came at last to a house, surrounded by trees. The car stopped at the gate. Janet looked at the house, it had a familiar air; she had that strange feeling "I have been here before."

As they went up the path, "I hope the Marches will be glad to see us," said Helen.

Then Janet knew. "The Marches? This isn't? That is——"

"Yes," Helen said. "It is Orchard House. Your friends Meg and Jo, Beth and Amy lived in it. You told me that they were your first link with America, so I planned to bring you here."

"I didn't know it was so near," Janet said. Everything in America, so it seemed to her, was vast distances away from everywhere else.

This house was not like any other one. In most homes families come and go, leaving little imprint of their personality. But here the presence of the family was deep-etched. There was the sofa with the pillow that Jo had used as a barrier between Laurie and herself. Beth's piano. The kitchen where Hannah had made turnovers and Jo had put salt on the strawberries. Upstairs, the girls' rooms with actual sketches made by Amy—you never could think of her as May Alcott but only as Amy March —on each side of the window. In the front hall, where one stood to bid the house a reluctant farewell, there seemed still the faint hope that the girls themselves would come down the stairs. Janet found herself wishing with fierce insistence that the one to come down would be Jo. Then she could ask her the question that was so often in her mind, "How did you really get *started* on a book?"

"The Marches have always been my friends," she said to Helen. "Ever since I first met them, on that rainy day in Trinidad. I wonder in how many homes in other countries they've stood for America."

"We couldn't have chosen a better family," Helen said. "They're American through and through." She said it as if the Marches—the Alcotts—were still alive. That, Janet thought, was how one felt about them. She closed the front door slowly as she went out.

Back at the Marshalls' house again, the enchantment of the day was broken by a post card that lay on the table in the hall. It was from Stephen. There was a rather feeble picture of the Brooklyn Bridge and the words, "To remind you of Brooklyn." It might or might not mean that he was missing her.

"Do you think I should write to him?" she asked Helen.

"No. If he can't do better than that mangy post card, I certainly wouldn't write. If he doesn't hear from you he'll be tickled to death to see you back."

"I wonder!" Janet said. Something told her all was not going well in Brooklyn. And, at that moment, what went on in Brooklyn was of more importance to her than the far-off battles of the war.

She counted the days until her return, marked them off on the calendar, but was at the same time afraid to go. At last came September and the beginning of the senior year.

Chapter 22

"Hearts don't break," Janet said gloomily. "They only crack into a thousand little pieces. If they broke it would be better—because then they wouldn't exist."

"And neither would you!" said Helen. They were sitting, cross-legged on the couch in Helen's room, weaving baskets. "Unfortunately, nobody's thought up any way, yet, for living without a heart. What is it, anyway? Having trouble with Stephen?"

"Trouble! More than that. It's all over."

"Too bad," Helen said. "Don and I are going to the movies tonight and we thought maybe you and Stephen would come along. What happened?" She put down her basket and lay back on the pillows to listen.

"I've been dying to tell you for days," Janet said. "I came back on a Sunday, you'll remember. I was glad it was a Sunday, because Stephen would be at home."

"Go on," encouraged Helen. "Wasn't he?"

"That was the trouble. When I got there they were all having supper. Tom's girl was there; she comes every Sunday." Janet paused.

"Well," said Helen, "you didn't mind Tom's girl being there, did you? Not getting to be a dog-in-the-manger?"

"No," said Janet. "I didn't mind Tom's girl. But, you see, Stephen's girl was there, too."

Helen sat bolt upright. "What did you say? *Stephen's girl?*"

"You heard me. *Stephen's girl.*"

"But I thought you——"

"Not any more. No wonder I didn't get letters from him during the summer. The minute I was out of the way he picked himself another girl."

"Gosh!" said Helen. "I'm sorry." She gave Janet a little hug. "Don't take it so hard"—for tears were dripping on the basket Janet was still trying to weave. "He isn't worth it."

"But I—I love him," Janet said. "And every Sunday I'm going to have to sit across the table from that girl. Stephen looks at her as if she were pure gold."

"What's she like?" asked Helen. "Pretty?"

"No, she's not much to look at. Lots of blond hair and rather pale blue eyes. I couldn't stand it if she were pretty. But she's an awfully good cook. I think that's how it started. Stephen's always saying, 'You ought to taste Lily's brownies' and 'Lily's chocolate cake, yum!' "

"H'm," said Helen. "Lily. She *would* be called something

like that. Chocolate cake. Brownies. As I remember, about all you can do in the way of cooking is to boil an egg."

"I can scramble them," sniffed Janet. "And I make cocoa beautifully."

"Cocoa and scrambled eggs," said Helen. "Not much of a help against brownies and chocolate cake. You'd better forget him."

"How can I?" Janet was more tearful than ever. "I live in the house with him, see him every day. And on Sundays I have to see them both."

"Let's forget him, now, anyway." Helen took the tear-splashed basket from Janet's hands. "You aren't much good at weaving. I'll work on your basket if you'll help me with my poem."

It was one of the crosses that the girls of the training school had to bear, this weekly making of a poem about some phase of child development. Unfortunately Froebel had made songs about such things and his followers were expected, at least in this particular school, to do it, too. Most of the girls found it difficult. Janet didn't mind. Rhyming came easily to her and she tossed off the verses—not poems, she knew that—in a carefree way that the other girls envied. Rhymes about a baby's supper, a mother bird bringing up her young, foolish rhymes made to order and as commonplace as the illustrations in a mail-order catalog.

"I've started the first verse," said Helen. "But it limps on all feet. Take a look at it."

"Pretty awful," Janet said. "Here, it should go like this—" and for a time, while she worked on the poem, Stephen went out of her mind.

Unfortunately, he kept coming back into it, and he simply would not be pushed out. Janet's school work suffered, and her grades went lower and lower. Miss Beck called her into the office.

"Janet," she said, eyes snapping. "What is the matter with your work? It's been falling off lately. Is it a love affair?"

"It isn't, now," Janet stated truthfully.

"But it was. I thought so. I've noticed the circles under your eyes. Do you know what I'm going to do for you?"

"No. I can't imagine."

"I'm going to put you in the most difficult kindergarten I can find. Let me see, where have you been teaching?"

Janet said, "In Lincoln kindergarten."

"How do you like it there?"

"I love it," Janet said. "And I hate to leave, I've grown so fond of the children."

"Good," said Miss Beck. "Some of our girls imagine they don't like to go to Lincoln because the children are Negro."

"I know," Janet nodded. "It was one of the things that surprised me when I came to America. In Trinidad we have a rather different feeling."

"British colonies seem to be a step in advance of us," said Miss Beck. "But *only* a step. There still are many difficulties. I'm sorry to take you away from Lincoln, but I'm going to send you to Greenhill—toughest children in Brooklyn and the dirtiest. You haven't been doing well in your practice teaching, and it's time you began to make good."

Janet rather welcomed the tough assignment. The kindergarten was in a slum district and the children were difficult. They *were* dirty, some of them actually sewed into their clothes for the winter. That problem she solved by putting the worst ones on the opposite side of the table, they weren't so bad at a distance. Apart from this they were delightful children, and Miss Stern, the director of the kindergarten, was particularly sympathetic.

It was a winter day, with the temperature well below zero, when she said to Janet: "Maggie hasn't been in kindergarten for a week. I wish you'd go over there and see what is the trouble."

"Over there" proved to be a shop that sold poultry. It was small and dark and smelly. Invited to "go back," Janet waded through a floorful of blood-spattered feathers, and finally arrived at a tiny, dark, back room. Maggie, a gnome-like child, was there. She welcomed her teacher with delight. Her mother was not quite so cordial.

"My Maggie no go kindergarten because she no lik' to go," she stated, defiantly.

"But she does," Janet objected. "She loves kindergarten. Don't you, Maggie?"

Maggie nodded. "My mother she no let me go. I no got coat."

The secret was out, and now that it was, Maggie's mother seemed relieved. And, when a coat was found for Maggie—a warm coat several sizes too large, in which she looked more gnome-like than ever—she never missed a day in kindergarten.

"But she looks as though she had grown up under glass," Janet said to Miss Stern. "Of course she doesn't get any sunshine in those dark, back rooms. And the shop is repulsive. I used to be sorry that some of the Negroes and Indians in Trinidad had to live in such poor houses, but at least they had lots of sunshine, and plenty of fruit to eat and flowers growing in their yards. Why do people have to live in slums? Why do cities allow it?"

"That's something I've never been able to answer," said Miss Stern. "Perhaps some day we'll work it out. No one should live in the kind of place Maggie lives in. This is your first experience in a *real* slum district, isn't it?"

"Yes," Janet said. "And Maggie's house has made me think."

The year went by, and at last it was June, with graduation very near. On a late afternoon the seniors assembled in the small garden. Miss Beck and most of the teachers had gone home, which was just as well for the girls' plans. They grouped themselves around one of the garden beds. Helen carried a spade, Janet a coffin-shaped box in which lay a small white china doll from the five-and-ten cent store.

"We are at the end of our senior year, about to bury The Child," announced the President of the class. They took turns digging a shallow grave. The box was placed in it and the President solemnly intoned:

"We now bid farewell to The Child who has been with us so constantly for two years. To this grave we commit The Child as we have known him in Child Psychology, in Diseases of Childhood, in all the other courses dealing with The Child. Ashes to ashes. Dust to dust."

The grave was filled in, and on the neat little mound the girls placed a handful of flowers. Laughing, they went back into the school.

There was now nothing but graduation, with its flurry of white dresses and American Beauty roses.

"This time I'm having the prettiest and most American dress I can find," Janet said. "I'm tired of made-over clothes that don't look in the least American, and I've only had two new dresses since I came."

It *was* a pretty dress. The Monroes were enthusiastically admiring.

"You look like a million," said Tom.

Stephen said nothing, but in the semi-darkness of the front hall he came up to her and looked so much as if he were going to kiss her that Janet drew away hastily and hurried to the door. He was there before her, holding it open, looking at her with peculiar intentness.

"Good-bye. Good luck!" he said.

Helen was waiting on the steps, and Janet, as she joined her and walked to the streetcar, was conscious that Stephen was still standing in the doorway, looking after them.

"Men!" Janet said fiercely. "I'm going to get myself a nice job in a girls' boarding school. Then I won't see a man from one year's end to another. I'm *through*."

"Don't fool yourself," said Helen. "This is only the beginning."

Chapter
23   THE SHINING
VALLEY

GENESEO WAS A delightful little town, perched on the hill overlooking the valley of the Genesee River. It was important to Janet because her first teaching position was there From the Normal School, which was on friendly terms with the valley, the streets climbed upward, each one a little steeper than the last, so that walking up them, one felt that the town must eventually climb all the way up to Heaven.

There were plenty of homes—it seemed a promising place to live. But appearances didn't mean much. Every room in every house was occupied by teachers or by students who had over-flowed the dormitories. The librarian of the school finally gave Janet a ray of hope.

"There's a room in the house where I board," she said. "It's a funny old-fashioned house, belongs to Mr. Bird, a widower. We call it Birdcage. The room isn't very big, but I think you'd like it. And you can have meals as well."

Any room, no matter what size, was a find. Janet settled down in it with a sigh of relief, unpacked her suitcases, hung her dresses in the one closet. A small room, but the window looked into a big maple tree where squirrels lived, and were constantly at war with the robins.

It was a queer household. Old Mr. Bird and his ancient house-keeper who obviously resented the fact that they must "let rooms" to the teachers. Two demonstration school teachers a little older than Janet. Martha Dunn, the librarian. Celia, a student who helped in the house for her board. But it was a place to live, and it was not too far from work.

To go to bed in a strange room, in a strange town, the night before starting one's first job—was ever anything so terrifyingly alone? The job in itself was frightening, for she was to be assistant in the demonstration kindergarten of the Normal School. Janet lay awake for a long time, thinking about the next day, and finally from the sheer exhaustion of too much bridge-crossing, fell asleep.

A slight rustling noise awoke her. It was morning and the sunlight slanted through the leaves of the maple tree, danced on the floor. And on her bed, right in the middle of the quilt, sat a gray squirrel. Paw on heart, he sat there calmly, looking at her with bright, questioning eyes. Janet made a slight move and, with a quick jerk of his tail, the squirrel was gone. On the window sill he paused a moment to look back at her, then leapt to a branch of the maple tree. It was a friendly beginning to a morning, and it helped. At least for a brief time it kept her from crossing any more bridges.

After breakfast, Martha walked down the hill to school with her, keeping up a brisk flow of conversation. "Here is the Big Tree Inn," as they crossed Main Street. "Named after the Indian village of Big Tree. Too bad New York State didn't keep even more of the old Indian names than it did. They had such lovely meanings: 'Where the Heavens lean against the Earth,' 'The place where the milkweed grows.' Think of naming a town Moscow when its name had meant 'Where the hemlock was spilled'!"

Janet was interested in spite of herself. They were halfway down the hill now, and Martha paused for a minute. "Look down at the valley," she said. "That's one name we kept, and that is utterly satisfying. Genesee—'the beautiful valley' or 'shining clear valley,' if you prefer. It's misty these September mornings, but in the spring you will find it 'shining and clear'."

In the spring! That seemed far away and there was, for Janet, only the present, with the school coming nearer every minute. Sensing this, Martha said: "The kindergarten room is one of the nicest rooms in the school. And Virginia Graham, with whom you'll work, is one of the jolliest teachers. You will enjoy it."

The demonstration kindergarten of the Normal School was a big, cheerful room. Virginia was the most charming girl in the world, with a kind, humorous mouth and laughing brown eyes. The children were delightful, though unusually lively. But Janet felt as if she had stepped into an entirely unfamiliar country. Virginia had been trained in the newer kindergarten methods—those that had been originated, to a great extent, by a teacher with vision whose name was Patty Smith Hill. Janet remembered that Miss Hill had lectured—once and once only— at her training school, and that Miss Beck had set her lips and made frigid remarks about these strange fly-by-night ideas that wouldn't last.

But they *were* lasting. They were sweeping the kindergartens all over the country. They dominated this particular kindergarten and Janet found herself quite unprepared to meet them. In this room there was no circle painted on the floor; the children gathered in an informal group. There were no colored balls on strings, or tiny blocks in boxes, such as Froebel had devised. Materials were *big*. There were big rubber balls, and huge blocks with which the children could build houses large enough to play in. Instead of sewing designs on cards, the children sewed on cloth, even made crude dresses for themselves. And they played with dolls! Most important of all, the teachers did not make day-by-day, week-by-week plans for the children. They followed the children's own interests, helped them to work these interests out in the best way. Janet was very much mystified by it all and felt herself inadequate. She didn't know how to use these strange materials; the children were more at home with them that she, consequently they took advantage of her. The only thing that was the same was storytelling—Janet clung to that as the survivor from a sinking ship clings to a raft. But the raft was small and the waves washed over her.

"I didn't know you'd had a strictly Froebelian training," Virginia Graham said. "It's a handicap in this type of kindergarten. And your discipline isn't all it should be. Sometimes I think you are afraid of the children. And, if you are, they always know it."

Days in kindergarten were miserable. Janet longed for them to be over, so that she could get back to the friendly atmosphere of Birdcage and tell her troubles to Martha. Martha, not knowing much about kindergarten, couldn't see how on earth a change of materials and methods could be so important, but she was sympathetic.

And, outside of her teaching, Janet was fairly happy. Geneseo was a friendly little town. Shyness kept her on the outer edge of school activities; she was a fascinated spectator—no more than that. It was not until Thanksgiving that things began to be different.

At Thanksgiving the school authorities decided to keep the students in Geneseo. There was an epidemic of infantile paralysis, and it seemed best not to allow visits to neighboring towns. When the news was broken, there was fierce and outspoken opposition.

"Stay here at school? Why, I've never been away from home at Thanksgiving."

"It's a gyp!"

"I'm going, anyway. My mother expects me."

The students gathered in groups and talked. Resentment ran high. Something had to be done about it. There was to be a large Thanksgiving dinner at the school. Members of the faculty contributed ideas as to how the day might be made a pleasant one. Some one suggested that students and faculty should come to the dinner dressed as Pilgrims or Indians. At first the students sniffed at the idea, then they began to think it might be fun. All over town Pilgrim and Indian costumes were in course of construction. Blankets were in tremendous demand, so were turkey feathers.

"We should have a story," Martha said. "Janet, you like to tell stories. Will you tell this one?"

"To the whole school?" Janet was incredulous. "You know I couldn't do *that*."

"*I* think you can. So far you haven't done a single thing for the students. And you could tell the story of Mary Jemison."

"But I don't know it. I don't know anything about her, except that she lived with the Indians in this valley."

"It's all in a book in the library. You can make it over into a story."

"It sounds simply impossible," Janet said. But curiosity took her on unwilling feet to the library, where she found the story in a small, old-fashioned book. It was told baldly, and without much color, as Mary Jemison herself had related it to the author. But the story shone through and fascinated Janet. Mary Jemison, "White Woman of the Genesee," had been carried off by the Seneca Indians when she was a little girl. They had brought her to the Genesee valley and had adopted her into the tribe. There she had lived all her life, had married an Indian chief, had refused to go back to her own people. It was a wonderful story and it was waiting to be told.

"And of course," Martha said, "you must wear Seneca Indian costume. Yes, I know you'd rather be a Pilgrim, that you think it's more in keeping with your personality. But I'll help you with the costume, and you'll like it when it's finished."

On Thanksgiving day the students streamed from each house and dormitory like ants from anthills. The streets were alive with white-capped Pilgrims and feathered Indians. Janet stood at the window of Birdcage watching the costumed figures go down the hill. "Oh, Martha, look! Dr. Davenport! I can't stand it!" For the dignified President of the school was walking down the street, a feather in his non-existent hair, edges of blanket showing coyly below his overcoat.

"If Dr. Davenport is going down, we'd better get started," Martha said, her round, ruddy face looking rounder than ever in a Pilgrim cap.

"I'm not going to be able to tell that story," Janet warned. "You may as well give up the idea. I'm so scared that I have a queer empty feeling where my stomach should be."

"That's not fright. That's hunger." Martha was brisk and definite. "A little turkey and you'll be feeling fine."

In spite of protests, in spite of queer feelings, Janet found herself walking down the hill with the others from Birdcage. A light snow had begun to fall, as if to complete the Thanksgiving picture. At the school the students were already gathered around the long tables which were cheerful with chrysanthemums and autumn leaves.

"Praise God from Whom all blessings flow." The voices of the students were fresh and young and earnest. Janet looked over the room as, with a rustle, they all sat down. Why, there were *thousands* of them—or so it seemed. The room stretched away into infinitude. When it came time for the story she was going to have the worst case of stage fright ever known. They would have to carry her out.

As dinner went on, she felt a little calmer. From where she sat she could look through the big windows to the valley, now powdered with snow. During the last week she had lived so constantly with the story that now it seemed to her she could see the long-houses of the Senecas. The squaws were dressing Mary Jemison in her Indian garments, exclaiming over her yellow hair. Janet could almost hear, instead of the buzz of table conversation, the chant with which the Indians had welcomed Mary into the tribe:

> *Deh-he-wä-mis has come;*
> *Then let us receive her with joy.*
> *She is handsome and pleasant,*
> *Oh, she is our sister and gladly*
> *We welcome her here.*

She had not known that the story had become such a part of her. How strange it was that she, the only one in the school who was not an American, should be bringing to them this charming story of their own valley! She would *have* to tell the story and tell it well.

And when she stood up to tell it, she knew that she could. In a clear voice that held only the slightest tremble, she began: "Many years ago there lived in the valley of the Genesee a tribe of Seneca Indians, of the Six Nations. The Great Hill People they were called, for it was said that they had come into the world by breaking out of the hill at the head of Canandaigua Lake . . ."

The students were listening. There was a little stir among those who came from Canandaigua. Janet went on: "And at the same time there was, in Pennsylvania, a family named Jemison. One of the daughters was Mary, and her hair was the color of corn tassels when the corn is ripe. . . ."

When the story was over the students crowded around, with

warm enthusiasm, to thank her. But nothing that was put into words was as great as the inner satisfaction of not having failed in her trust. After that it was easier to be a part of things, to join in student activities.

Winter came swirling down from the Great Lakes, piling the snow up in tremendous banks. It was after one of the big snow-storms that Janet found herself selected to chaperon a straw-ride. She didn't know what a straw-ride was, but she was game to try one. As for being a chaperon, she was the youngest member of the faculty, not much older than the students, younger than those who had already taught and had come back to get a higher certificate. That, had she known it, was exactly why they had asked her to go with them. And, as two chaperons were required, they had chosen a very young man who taught physics in the High School. Janet had noticed him, one couldn't help noticing his red curly hair and brown eyes. He reminded her of her cousin Jock; who, the year before, had marched off to the skirl of bagpipes and who had died in Flanders. But this man's name was Hank, a name as American as any she had heard.

The sleigh was a big farm wagon on runners; it held twenty-two of them. Sturdy farm horses pulled it, bells jingled and it was all very gay. The first part of the ride went well; they sped along the well-cleared road with its snowbanks piled high at the sides. Out in the open country the road was rougher, the drifts higher. The sleigh jounced over the frozen snow and—suddenly without warning—the whole top tipped off the runners and collapsed into a snowbank. Janet felt it going, it was a curious sensation to be suspended in the air for a moment. Then she was down under a tangle of bodies and legs and arms—suffocating—pushing—struggling—her mouth full of snow.

The students managed to pick themselves out of the snow, one by one. Some of the girls who had been near the bottom of the heap were sobbing. One was having hysterics, all by herself, on a snowbank. Janet pulled herself up into a sitting position.

"If you wouldn't mind getting off my stomach," said a feeble, gasping voice, "I think I could breathe."

Janet looked down. Sure enough, she was sitting on Hank. She scrambled off and Hank sat up, breathing deeply and wiping the snow off his glasses.

"Whew! It's no fun to be the bottom of the pile. Listen, hadn't we better do something about Esther? We can't let her go on having hysterics out here in the snow."

They took the laughing, crying Esther to a nearby farmhouse, where the farmer's wife made tea for her and she gradually calmed down and made only small, whimpering sounds.

"I think we'd better finish the party at school," said Hank. "They've got the top on the sleigh now, but I notice the horses are turned towards home. It's too rough to go on, even the driver thinks so."

They piled back into the sleigh, fair, fluffy Esther getting sympathetic attention from the boys, which was what she had hoped for all along.

When the party was over, Hank walked up with Janet to Birdcage.

"Tell me," she said as they went up the hill, "is your name really Hank? I thought Americans were only called Hank in books."

"My name is Henry," he said, "and there are lots of Hanks outside of books."

"And Hirams and Seths?"

"And Hirams and Seths. They are good old names. By the way, how would you like to go coasting tomorrow? I can get a sled, and it's fun to coast down the long hill."

Janet had never coasted, but, again, she was willing to try. The hill was almost a mile long and coasting down was magnificent, walking up not quite so good. By the end of the afternoon she felt that she knew Hank quite well, for, pulling the sled up the long hill, there was plenty of time to talk. Hank was off girls, he assured her, one having heartlessly turned him down. With Janet feeling much the same way about men, they agreed that there was to be friendship but absolutely nothing more between them, no romantic nonsense—the phrase was Hank's.

"Do you like teaching?" Janet asked on the second trip up the hill.

"Sure I do," said Hank. "Why?"

"Because I was wondering if I did. So far I can't decide. I do know there's something wrong and I'm not enjoying it."

"Isn't there *any* part of it you enjoy?"

"Oh, yes, telling stories. I love that."

Hank stopped pulling the sled, stood still in the snow and looked at her. "Why, you're the one who told the story of Mary Jemison at Thanksgiving. You're just the person we need at the settlement house down in the valley. You know, there's a little settlement house down there—it takes care of the kids belonging to the Italian workers in the vineyards. I work with the boys and we need some one to start a story-hour. The students can help. I was going to speak to the head of your department about it—now I'll just tell her I want *you* to do it. Will you?"

"I'd love to," said Janet. "If I can—" Already she was beginning to have doubts, as she always did when anything new presented itself.

"Of course you can. See here, we've coasted long enough. You look frozen. The people in that little house at the top of the hill are friends of mine. Let's go in and sit by their fire—and talk some more about this."

Chapter
24   "SOME THINGS I CAN DO"

THE FIRST story-hour came and Janet found herself alone in the small settlement house with two students. All primed with stories for the smallest ones, they were even more nervous than she. But the children came in joyously and soon they were gathered around the three story-tellers. Janet had the older group. They were good listeners, but as the story went on, she found herself telling it to one boy only. He had pushed in a little ahead of the others and sat forward on his chair, his clasped hands hanging loosely between his knees. His black eyes never wavered, his face mirrored every mood of the story. When it was all over and the children filed out, he lingered and stood there shifting from one foot to another. Finally he spoke.

"Teacher," he said, "I liked that story fine. You coming next week?"

"Yes," said Janet. "I'm glad you liked it. What is your name?"

The boy's face clouded. "Jake," he said, and was out of the door like a flash. Janet was puzzled.

"Benny," she said to one of the students who taught regularly at the settlement, "do you know that boy?"

Benny nodded. "I'll say I do! Jake's the terror of the neighborhood. Been expelled from the public school twice—I shivered when I saw him come in. They threw him out again last week."

"Heavens!" said Janet. "It's a good thing I didn't know. Anyway, he's crazy about stories. I don't think he'll give us any trouble."

The story-hour had been a success! Janet went home in a warm glow, for here was one thing she *could* do. But the next week things did not go so well.

Everything started peacefully. Janet was well launched on her story, Jake was listening with an intensity that almost frightened her, when—rattle, bang, rattle, bang, crash!

"Stones on the roof," Jake said out of the corner of his mouth. "Don't notice, teacher, go on with the story."

Janet tried, but again it came; rattle, bang, crash, rattle, bang!

"Jake, do you know anything about this?"

"It's my gang," admitted Jake. "They don't like I should listen to stories in here."

"Oh!" said Janet. "Wait a minute, children, this has to stop." She heard her voice saying the bold words, but her knees were trembling. She went to the door and opened it. The boys, stones poised, stood looking at her.

"Boys," she said, in a voice considerably smaller than she would have liked it to be, "don't you want to come in?"

The gang shouted with laughter.

"Stories is for little kids," one big boy said. "We ain't little kids." He gave a signal and a whole shower of stones fell on the roof. One bounced off dangerously near to Janet. She retreated. It was safer inside.

"You can't do nothing with 'em," remarked Jake, who had been an interested spectator. "They're tough."

"Jake!" said Janet desperately. "*I* can't, but *you* can. It's your gang and you've got to do it."

"Aw, nuts," grumbled Jake. "I can't do nothing with 'em."

"You can, too. Listen to me, Jake. If you want stories you've *got* to do it."

"Do what?"

"Go out there and tell them to come in. They'll listen to you."

"Like fun they will."

"You can do it. Go out and tell them that if they'll come in I'll tell them a story that isn't for little kids—a good story—a real boy's story. Jake, you've *got* to do it."

"All right," said Jake. "But if I get a stone on my bean—" He ambled to the door, opened it and looked out.

"Say, fellers, lay off, will you? This teacher here, she's all right. And she says come in and she'll tell you a he-man story."

There was a burst of laughter but no more stones.

"Aw, come on in, fellers. C'm *on*!"

The gang conferred. Janet, knowing that they were coming in, felt the cold sweat breaking out all over her. They were coming—in a moment they would be marching up the steps—and she must produce a he-man story. She didn't know any! What was she to do? She thought over all the stories she knew, thought fast and feverishly. They all seemed pretty frilly and didn't fit the occasion in the least.

The sound of heavy shoes coming up the steps. Something must be done—must be done—the words sang themselves into a refrain in her mind. Then she knew. Why, of course! She'd try that, and if it didn't work, it didn't work, that was all. When the door opened and the boys—only six of them—trooped in, she was ready. Her own story group she handed hastily over to Benny.

"Sit here, boys. The big chairs, not those little ones. Jake, you come with us."

Now she must begin! Her hands were clammy, but she launched bravely into the story. How fortunate it was that the book of Norse tales had been such a favorite of her childhood! Good old solid Norse myths! Grand stories with a floor under them. Not her first choice for Italian boys, of course, but the best she could do. Would they listen?

In a voice that shook a little she began the story of Thor and his hammer. It worked like a charm! Seven pairs of eyes were fixed on her now. Her voice steadied, the story went on to a triumphant climax.

"Gee! That's some story!"

"Can we come next week?"

"Tell us another like that. Got any more about that guy, Thor?"

"Gee, he was some guy!"

Janet could scarcely believe her good fortune. In the weeks that followed she worked harder than she had ever worked before, memorizing stories that would hold the gang. And the charm continued to work all the way through the heroes of Asgard, Greek hero tales and Paul Bunyan. "Though I wish you'd find some good Westerns to tell them," said Hank.

Meanwhile, Janet and Benny were organizing a play with the children a little younger—the parents could come to that and see some tangible results of the story-hour. The children's choice was Cinderella. That was fine, for it was in Janet's very recent experience. After the gang had left she called the children to her.

"If we're going to give this play we've got to choose parts. Who wants to be Cinderella?"

A dozen hands went up. That was easy.

"Who wants to be the prince?" Not a hand.

"Doesn't anybody want to be the prince?"

A small boy spoke up. "I don't wanna be no prince. I wanna be a rat."

"A rat?"

"One of them what turned into a footman—*you* know."

The rats were duly cast. Still no prince.

Then Jake, who had lingered on the outskirts of the group, stepped forward.

"How about me for the prince?"

Janet caught her breath. She looked at Jake—in all his toughness, one black lock straggling down over his eye, a cut on his lip from his last fight, dirt ingrained in every visible square inch of him. Why, Jake *couldn't* be the prince. It would ruin the play.

She opened her mouth to say No! Then in a flash it came to her. The play didn't matter, Jake did. And if he felt like a prince inside, what of the outer shell? She put her hand on his shoulder.

"All right, Jake. You shall be the prince. We'll start rehearsals next week. And you might wash your hands just a little—run over them quickly before you come."

"Aw, nuts," said Jake.

No one knew why the gang didn't kid Jake about his princehood—they simply didn't. Apparently it was taken for granted —for Jake, though tough, was younger than any of the other boys and they were inclined to be lenient with him. The play was a great success, though Jake in a pale blue costume with ostrich plumes in his cap was a living, walking anachronism. Jake, shining with soap, scrubbed to the ears, kneeling to kiss the hand of Cinderella.

After the play Jake's very Italian mother (he had a Jewish father, which accounted for his name) came up to Janet and held out a hand no cleaner than Jake's—at least than Jake's on ordinary occasions.

"I thank you for what you do for my boy," she said. "Jakie good boy. Teacher at school say he bad, but she no know my Jakie."

Janet agreed. "Jake's a good boy. He just needs to be kept busy. I'll go to the school and talk to them—maybe they'll let him go back. They can do anything with him if they keep him busy enough."

Hank, who had come to see the play, walked home with Janet. The almost-melted patches of snow crunched pleasantly under their feet.

"You did a perfectly grand job," he said. "Where did you get the idea that you can't do things?"

"Some things I *can* do," Janet said. "But teaching isn't one of them. I'm not a good teacher—and that's that."

"Bunk," snorted Hank. "You've got some kind of complex about it. Get over it!"

Chapter
25 "OF WOUNDS AND SORE DEFEAT"

THE NEXT MONTH everything went to pieces. Spring was in the air, the kindergarten children were restless, nothing Janet could do would make them settle down. Virginia sighed over it sympathetically, but with a growing weariness.

"You just don't know what it's all about, Janet. You didn't have the right training for our type of work, and that's that. You don't know how much freedom to give or where to call a halt. The children walk all over you and I don't know what to do about it."

With a heavy weight choking her throat, pressing down on her stomach, Janet went to the library. She couldn't go home— it wasn't three o'clock—but she could sit there peacefully and get herself together a little.

Martha looked up as she came in. "What's the matter?" she asked. "You look as if you'd lost your last friend." She stamped a date briskly and handed the book to an outgoing student.

"Everything's wrong." Janet's tone was so desperate that Martha looked at her sharply, then called a library student to take her place at the desk.

"Come into my office. You may as well spill over. What's happened?" Not the headlines? I know how you feel when London is bombed."

"No, I haven't seen a paper," said Janet "and nothing special has happened except to me. It's simply that Virginia says I'm no good. There's something wrong, but I don't know just what it is. Anyhow, I can't teach. Guess I'll give up and scrub floors."

"Idiot!" said Martha. "You've got the stuff in you. Don't be yellow. Why don't you *do* something about it? Go down to Columbia, take a course, take your college degree, find out what it's all about. Don't let it get you! *Do* something."

"It *has* got me," Janet said. "I don't want to do anything. I just want to crawl into a hole and die. I thought I could be a teacher and I can't."

"That's silly talk." An edge came into Martha's voice. "The whole trouble is you have no confidence in yourself. You've got to find that, somehow, because you'll never be any good until you do."

"I'll never be any good, anyway. I'm a failure—a flat, fizzled-out failure."

"Well," said Martha, "I'll say you aren't a failure. No one who can do what you did with that story-hour is a failure. But you are a coward if you won't face things. You aren't facing them now. You're just being awfully sorry for yourself. Your words say, 'I'm a failure.' Inside you're saying, 'I'm a poor misunderstood creature. Nobody appreciates me.' Listen—go over by the window and read for a while—then let's walk home together. We've got to thrash this thing out."

They went out of the office into the pleasant library room. Janet walked slowly over to a table in the window, and sat where she could look out over the valley. The window was open and the warm spring wind blew the curtains aside. The trees were softly, newly green. It might have been a beautiful world to any one else, but again, as on the day that Father died, Janet saw it all in tones of gray—there was no color in it anywhere. Because she could not bear to look at it, she went to the nearest stack and chose a book—just any book—at random. It would do to sit and look busy with. She couldn't settle down to reading, but one couldn't just sit in a library indefinitely and stare.

The book proved to be a poem by William Vaughn Moody. Of all things! thought Janet, idly turning the pages. If there's anything I don't need just now, it's poetry. As the pages flipped over, her eyes caught a first line: *Of wounds and sore defeat*— Sore defeat! That was it! Maybe she'd better find out what some one else had to say about it. She began to read.

> *Of wounds and sore defeat*
> *I made my battle stay;*
> *Winged sandals for my feet*
> *I wove of my delay;*
> *Of weariness and fear*
> *I made my shouting spear;*
> *Of loss, and doubt and dread*
> *And swift oncoming doom;*
> *I made a helmet for my head*
> *And a floating plume.*
> *From the shutting mist of death,*
> *From the failure of the breath*
> *I made a battle horn to blow*
> *Across the vales of overthrow.*
> *Oh, harken, love, the battle horn!*
> *The triumph clear, the silver scorn.*
> *Oh, harken, where the echoes bring*
> *Down the gray disastrous morn,*
> *Laughter and rallying!*

There was a peculiar, almost startling fitness to the words. She read them again, closed the book, sat looking out over the valley. Martha was putting on her hat. She came to the table and touched Janet on the shoulder.

"Come on! I'm ready. Get your things and we'll start. And let's get to the bottom of the matter—it can't go on like this."

They walked up the hill to Birdcage, the first half of the way in silence because Martha wanted Janet to speak first. Finally Janet burst out: "You were right, Martha. I'm a coward. I haven't faced all the reasons for failure, but I'm going to. It isn't only that I don't know how to work in this type of kindergarten. I'm self-conscious. I'm afraid of the children. I've *got* to get over that."

"I know," said Martha. "But I think when you're sure of yourself, when you really find out how to do things, confidence will come. Anyway, try a year at Columbia and see what it does for you. Then if you can't teach, try something else. But there's so much to teaching that isn't just being able to run one kindergarten like clockwork. Teaching's a most elastic profession. There must be a place in it for you."

"I'll write for the catalog tonight," said Janet as they went up the steps of Birdcage. "Honestly, Martha, you don't know how different things look to me."

Martha, her key in the door, stared at her unbelievingly.

"Why, I didn't say very much," she protested. "How did you start feeling that way?"

"It was partly you and partly a poem," said Janet. "Here, let me open the door, and when we get inside I'll explain."

That night Janet wrote to Columbia University for the catalog and when it came she made her decision. The training school work counted for two years, Janet found; in two more years she could have a degree. She would have to teach in between, because college would be expensive, and she would have to earn something before she could go on. But it would be only two years, instead of four as she had supposed. The decision was helped by the fact that a letter from Helen announced that she, too, felt the need of more training and was planning to take the year at Columbia. Helen went on to say that, if Janet would come, too, they could live in the college dormitory and take many of the same classes. It would be fun.

Janet told Hank about it one afternoon when they had walked up to the woods at the top of the hill. The freshness of spring was in the air and Janet had picked handsful of trillium and dog-toothed violets.

"Hank," she said, "next spring I'll be in New York. No trillium there. It's such a lovely flower and I'd never seen it until I came here."

"New York!" Hank was startled. "You're not leaving Geneseo?"

"Yes. I'm going to Columbia."

"Not running away? Not giving up too easily?"

"No. But I can't go on teaching without knowing more about it."

"I'll miss you, Jan," said Hank. "Like everything."

"And I'll miss you," Janet said. They walked down the hill swinging hands. It was the first time they had done anything like that.

Chapter
26
SIGNPOSTS AND
SLEEPING PILLS

THE COLLEGE DORMITORY was a buzz of voices. Laughter floated in and out of the rooms. Looking into the little cubicles, it was impossible to see how most of them would ever be in any sort of order. Beds were piled high with the contents of trunks and suitcases; there were piles even on the floor.

Janet was completely lost among her possessions. After a feeble struggle, she left the chaos that was her room to go into Helen's. It was in complete order, clothes hung in the closet or folded in bureau drawers, books neatly placed on shelves.

"Helen, I don't see how you do it! I haven't any system and I don't believe I'll ever find places for everything in such a small room. Anyway, I'm bored to death trying. I want to explore a little, to see what the place looks like."

"I'm just as curious as you are," Helen said. "Let's go out and look around. We never did get over here when we were in Brooklyn."

They went out of the dormitory and walked along the block to Teachers College, the School of Education of the University. The building was a red-brick one, standing flush with the street. Janet looked at it with some disappointment. "Not very romantic! Not like Girton, or like any ideas I've had of college. A few trees or a patch of grass would help!"

"But the campus is pretty," Helen said, looking across the

wide street to the Green. "Suppose we walk up and see the rest of the University. That will give us an idea of the place."

The University buildings, grouped around a red-brick quadrangle, were dignified and attractive in their plainness. Janet read the name on the Library: " 'King's College in the City of New York.' " That makes me feel at home. And the flag—that's even more English!" She looked up at the flagstaff from which floated Columbia's pale blue flag with its white crown—a legacy from the days when the University had been King's College.

The girls walked down the broad steps in front of the Library. In the center of the steps, looking down at the fountain, sat a very solid bronze lady, a book on her lap.

"Alma Mater!" Helen said. "Let's look for the owl. One of the girls told me about it."

They peered among the folds of the bronze skirts. "Here it is!" Janet had found it under one of the folds. The small bronze owl looked out at them solemnly.

"It makes her seem a little more approachable," Helen said. "But she's an awfully massive gal! By the way, the same student told me about the ghost."

"Ghost? What do you mean?"

"They say there's a ghost in the underground passage that runs from the Library to Teachers College. Don't think your English universities have all the atmosphere! Wouldn't you love to meet a college ghost?"

"Depends. On the kind of ghost. If it's a crabby old professor, no. If it's a young, good-looking ghost, maybe."

Helen thought it over. "Are ghosts ever good-looking? I've heard this one is young. But maybe we'd better leave him for another time. I'd like to walk over to the river, wouldn't you?"

Two days later classes began. The girls found that they were together in the educational classes, while for the academic ones they had different requirements. The first class was with Professor Patty Hill.

"I can hardly wait to see her," Janet said as they sat in the classroom. "Do you remember the day she came to Clark with all her dolls and playthings—and how shocked Miss Beck was? I had a grand time that day but I can't remember just how Miss Hill looked. I know she had oodles of personality."

There was a stir among the students. Professor Hill was arriving. She came into the room with quick steps, a tall, well-built woman with gray hair and a blue dress that exactly matched her eyes. For a minute she stood looking down at the class, sizing it up with her keen look. Then she smiled, a jolly, infectious smile that made them all smile back and be instantly at ease. When she spoke there was a trace of Southern accent.

"I could listen to her all day," Janet said. The students all felt the same way. From Kentucky and Texas, from California and Kansas, and from all over the world, they had come to study with this woman who had dared to change the whole kindergarten system. She had a way of making education a living thing. The knots into which over-serious students had tied themselves were loosed as she stood there, hands on hips, head thrown slightly back, eyes twinkling, and told stories that made even the most solemn student break into spontaneous laughter. From there she swung into the most serious of discussions. The class hung on every word.

"I begin to understand things better, already," Janet said as the class was dismissed. "She makes teaching so very human. And she makes you feel that children are *people*."

She understood even more when she and Helen sat and watched the children at work in the big sunny kindergarten room.

"Miss Brownell has such good times with the children," Janet said. "And no trouble with discipline. She seems to expect the right thing and to get it."

Helen looked puzzled. "I've never had any difficulty with the children. I love teaching, and I have good times with them, too. I think the trouble with you is that you began thinking in terms of 'discipline' and never got over it. You're all tangled up in discipline and theory like a kitten in a ball of wool. Forget it!"

"I'll try," Janet said meekly. "And I'm learning a lot in Miss Hill's class. It's funny how some classes are the kind you go to sleep in, and others give you real direction."

"Like signposts," Helen said. She chuckled. "Signposts and sleeping pills!"

" 'The Place of the Teacher in the Community,' " Janet said. "That's a sleeping pill if ever there was one. Tomorrow we have to go with that class to observation in the kindergarten. We won't get much out of it."

She was mistaken. After the observation, when the students went back to their classroom, the discussion was dull for a while. Then a young man with a smug expression said: "I objected to something that was going on in that room and I have been talking to some of the class about it. Perhaps you did not notice the little nun who was so industriously trying to convert the children to her religion?"

There was a silence. Then the professor said, and his voice had had a peculiar note in it: "Perhaps you will make yourself clearer?"

"I shall be very glad to," said the young man. "At the work-bench there was a nun, a practice teacher, obviously, and she did nothing for a very long time but help the children make small wooden crosses. It was very easy to do—just a matter of hammering two pieces of wood together—and when the children went home they took the crosses with them. Christians and Jews, and a Chinese child who might have belonged to an-other religion, they took the crosses with them."

There was silence again. Janet and Helen looked at each other, wonderingly. Then the professor said, his words clipped and cold: "There are possibly those in this room who could ex-plain this thing to you. But it would be better to go straight to the source. We will ask the Sister herself to come here and ex-plain it. Then there can be no question in your mind."

The little nun, round-faced and wide-eyed, was nervous when she came into the room. The professor was gentle with her.

"Sister Felicia," he said. "We have watched you at work and we think that you are a good teacher. But there is a young man here who insists that you were abusing the privileges of a prac-tice teacher. He says"—the professor passed a hand over his mouth—"that you spend your time teaching the children to make crosses, which, he suggests, has something to do with your religion. Will you tell him what you were doing?"

The students sat forward in their chairs.

The Sister was more wide-eyed than ever. For the moment, she was puzzled. And then she began to laugh. She laughed silently and her whole body shook with laughter. Then she stopped laughing and looked at the young man and said: "If you had known a little more about kindergarten, and if you had been a little less ready to be prejudiced, you would have seen more clearly. For those were not crosses we were making. They were airplanes."

"Airplanes!" The young man's voice was sharply challenging.

"Yes," said Sister Felicia. "One piece for the fuselage and one for the wings. That is how small children are apt to make their first airplanes."

"Thank you," said the professor. "That is all we need. And it is a fine example of how lack of understanding may start a rumor that will grow and grow until it is a large and dangerous thing. Not so long ago, in Long Island, I saw a tiny curl of smoke by the side of the road. I stopped the car and put out the little flame, because it might soon have become a forest fire. What you have just seen was a little blaze that had the same possibilities. They may start, these little fires, in your classroom or your community and they are your responsibility. Perhaps your greatest responsibility as a teacher."

"I'll never forget that class," Janet said to Helen as they went out of the room.

"Nor I," said Helen.

English classes, especially Appreciation of Poetry, were bright spots in the day. Professor Kern loved poetry and he transmitted that love to his students. Gray-haired, with a slight stoop and humorous eyes behind bone-rimmed glasses, he approached poetry as if it were part of life, not something off by itself. Instead of calling the roll he had his own method of asking each student to write out a few lines of a poem. Some liked it and some took it with groans and complaints.

There was a day when the professor asked Janet to stay for a moment after class. "I'm interested in your roll call," he said, picking up the paper on which she had written lines by Davies:

What is this life if, full of care,
We have no time to stand and stare?

No time to stand beneath the boughs
And stare as long as sheep and cows.

No time to see, when woods we pass,
Where squirrels hide their nuts in grass,

No time to see in broad daylight,
Streams full of stars, like skies at night.

* * * *

A poor life this, if full of care,
We have no time to stand and stare.

"Last week it was Housman and before that it was Herrick's "A Ternarie of Littles." I don't get those very often. And I've noticed your papers; they are very well done. Have you ever tried to write?"

Janet nodded. "I wrote stories, but just stories for children."

"Not *just* stories for children," Professor Kern said. "Some of the best writing has been done for them. And to write a book for children that will live even a few years, one must put into it all that goes into the writing of an adult book."

"I know that," Janet said. "But some people think writing for children is easy."

"Why did you stop writing? Teaching kill your creative spirit?"

"No, not that. I was too busy or something." She hesitated, then went on. "I wasn't very good at teaching and I spent my days struggling to keep my head above water. If I'd taken time off to write, I'd have drowned completely."

"Possibly not," said Professor Kern. "Possibly not. At any rate, you'd better start writing again. You've got it in you. And don't let yourself get too busy to see things and to write about them. Don't ever let that happen." He looked at her steadily, half smiling, and quoted under his breath the words he had just read back to her:

> "*A poor life this, if full of care,*
> *We have no time to stand and stare.*"

Janet went out of the room with a strange elation all through her. This was exactly what she needed, a little encouragement, a little direction. As soon as the college year was over and she had a job, she would try to write. She did not know, then, that she would be kept so busy in other ways that writing would be pushed into the background. First Aid—knitting—Liberty Loan drives—all these would have first call on leisure time. For, in the spring of that year, the United States went into the war.

Chapter
27 RESPONSIBILITIES

It was a spring day and Janet had taken her first-grade children to pick violets. That was one of the many nice things about this country day-school on the Philadelphia main line, one could be out-of-doors so much. The day was so warm and sunny that Janet and the children had moved the tables and chairs out under the trees. And, at the end of the arithmetic period, they had walked down to the woods for what the school catalog called "nature study," but what was really living for a time with trees and birds and flowers. At the foot of the school grounds was a strip of woodland that had been a joy all year. In the fall the children had collected the colored leaves, had rustled through them and dived headlong into the brown piles. In the winter they had made a Christmas tree for the birds. Now the wild apple trees tossed their pink blossoms into the little pond, violets were thick on the banks, and the children hunted for the white flowers that the May apples hid under their green umbrellas. As they picked violets, the children broke spontaneously into the song that Janet had taught them:

> *All the birds have come again,*
> *Come with joyous singing . . .*

Fair-haired Kurt led the song, he had the best voice in the group. Suddenly Janet realized that he was not singing in English. She held her breath. Would the children notice it? Anything might happen if they did.

For a moment they listened. Then: "He's singing in German!" said Donald. "Kurt is singing in German."

"Kurt's singing German! Kurt's singing German!" It ran like wildfire through the group. Little girls joined in shrilly, "Kurt's singing German!" Kurt stood back against a tree, his mouth set in a tight line, his face flushed to the roots of his yellow hair.

"Kurt's singing German! Kurt's singing German!" The mocking chant went on. Kurt dropped the violets that were in his hands and clenched his fists.

168

"Children," Janet said quickly. "Aren't you being rather silly? What if Kurt *did* sing in German? You know that his father is an American, but he came from Germany and he has taught Kurt the songs he sang when he was a little boy."

"We're fighting the Germans," one of the boys said. "Dirty Germans. Boches!" He gave a defiant look at Kurt.

"Yes, we are," Janet said. "But we're not fighting a song. Think how silly it would be to fight a song!" The laughter in her voice was a flame that ran through the group as quickly as the mocking chant had run. The words passed from child to child, "Silly to fight a song!"

With one of the quicksilver changes of childhood, Donald turned to Kurt. "Race you back to school, Kurt!" They were off, all of them, laughing and shouting, with Kurt and Donald in the lead.

Janet followed more slowly. She could let them go like that, be sure she would find them waiting calmly for her when she arrived. She thought of the day when she had first come to this school. Even though she was all fortified with methods and half a college degree, she had been far from sure of herself.

Miss West, the principal had changed all that. "You have good recommendations," she said. "And I don't believe this note about 'poor discipline.' You look as if you would have fun with the children. Did I tell you when I wrote that you would have charge of the two first grades?"

"Two first grades! Does that mean I have to teach both of them?"

"Don't be alarmed! The other teacher is a Vassar girl—Betty Wainwright. She will teach her own grade, but she's never had any teacher-training and I'm counting on you to help her. Technically she's your assistant. You will be responsible for planning the work with her."

Janet's head spun. Responsible for two grades! An assistant! It was fantastic.

"I'll do my best," she said. "But, honestly, I don't think I'm very good."

"Leave that for me to find out," said Miss West. "I think you'll come through."

And on this spring day Janet decided that she *had* come through. She and Betty had worked it out together. The children had learned to work together, too, and they had learned to read. All, that is, except Florence. A scrawny little girl with fair, straight hair and a stubborn mouth, a spoiled little girl who always wanted attention, Florence was definitely not a reader. Confronted by such a simple word as *cat*, she looked at it defiantly and said *dog*.

Today Janet wondered what she was going to do with Florence. She had tried everything and nothing had worked. The children were waiting for her at the tables under the trees, pushing their wet hair back with grimy hands.

"You will have to go in and wash your hands," Janet said. "And put your violets in water. Can I trust you to go in without me?"

When they had gone, she brought a pile of new books from a table on the school porch, and put one at each place. It would be fun to see their faces when they came back. They came demurely, the burden of responsibility resting on them, hands scrubbed and clean.

Then as they saw the books, they broke into a run. "Books!" they shouted. "New books!"

"Are they new primers?" asked Kurt, who was one of the best readers.

"New *first readers*," Janet said. "You can read well enough for those, now."

First readers! The wonder of it! The children took the books in their hands, sniffing them, as they always did a new book, with delight. They ran their hands lovingly over the stiff bindings, then turned the pages eagerly to see the pictures. Janet shared their excitement. They were keys, these books, keys to *Alice in Wonderland,* to the old fairy tales and *The Wind in the Willows.*

"I can read the first page!" "So can I." "Let me have the first turn?" The voices bubbled over with eagerness. Only Florence held the book in her hands and stared at it with blank eyes. What *was* to be done about her?

At the end of the year Florence was reluctantly promoted to second grade. There seemed to be no point in keeping her back.

"I think she's just going to grow up illiterate," Janet said to Betty Wainwright. "I *felt* illiterate when I went to take out the first papers for my citizenship a week ago. They asked me if I could read and write!"

"What did you say?" Betty asked.

"I was very dignified and said, 'I've been to college.' And the man looked at me and said: 'Lady, I asked you a question, *Can you read and write?* So I was very meek and said, 'I *think* so,' and that made him madder than ever."

Betty laughed. "You didn't tell me you'd taken out your first papers. I thought you hadn't decided whether you wanted to be an American."

"I haven't. But first papers aren't final, they leave one free to decide. And they will be there if I want to take the next step."

"Which I hope you will," said Betty. "We'd like you to be one of us."

The next year Janet wondered how she had ever been afraid of children. Teaching was fun. Telling stories was still the best thing in the world, but there was a real thrill in teaching the children to read; to write in first large straggling letters.

One day she went into the second-grade room to see how her last year's children were getting along. They could read well, she knew that. Florence had been her only failure. As she went into the room she heard a familiar voice. In the front row stood Florence, pleased and proud. Book in hand, she was reading fluently. It was only a primer, but Florence sailed through it. "The gingerbread boy ran away," Florence's voice went on in a magnificent sweep. Janet dropped into a chair to listen. Her legs simply wouldn't hold her up.

"How did you ever teach Florence to read?" she asked the second-grade teacher afterwards.

The second-grade teacher's eyes twinkled. "I didn't. You taught her. She came to my grade reading."

"I give up," said Janet. "What do you suppose . . ."

"I think she could read a little all the time," the second-grade teacher said. "But she got more attention from you when you thought she couldn't. That was all!"

Part 4

NEW HORIZONS

*N*EW HORIZONS

Chapter
28 *THE SILVER PENCIL*

IN NOVEMBER, the Armistice was signed. The papers carried the news in staring headlines. Cities and towns and villages went wild with joy. The air was filled with snowstorms of torn paper; strangers hugged each other in the streets. The war was over! There would never be another one.

The children were brimming over with excitement; Janet found herself very much out of patience with them. Lately her patience had been running thin. Renny, a nervous boy who simply could not sit still, annoyed her. And even the Armistice did not make her as happy as the rest of the joy-delirious world. Something must be the matter.

Each day she grew more tired and nervous, and then the pain began. At first it was only in her feet and ankles if she stood too long. Then it was in her knees and in her fingers. Finally she found that she could not walk.

"Is it rheumatism?" she asked the doctor. "I'm not old enough for that?"

"Arthritis," the doctor said. "You will have to go into a hospital for rest and treatment."

Rest! The word was a relief. But where was the money to come from? If she gave up her work her very small salary would stop, and then there would be nothing to pay the hospital expenses.

Fortunately Miss West came to the rescue. "We will pay your

salary until the end of the school year," she said. "And I can get you a free room in a hospital, because my father used to be superintendent of that hospital. They have a certain number of rooms kept for people who really can't afford to pay."

Every one was amazingly kind. In an emergency, then, Americans didn't only promise things. They *did* them. When one was really in trouble words meant exactly what they said, even more than they said. One week later, Janet was in the hospital. The free room was a dreary little cell, painted an unattractive drab color, with a single window that looked out on a court. But that first week it seemed like Heaven. She could lie there, could sleep all she wanted to, be relieved of all responsibility. She did not have to think, through continuous, gnawing pain, of the development of Renny and nineteen other children. She did not have to force herself to smile and play "Farmer in the Dell" when all she wanted was to sit down and take the weight off her feet.

After the first week, when she was rested and her nerves were quiet, the drab little room was not so pleasant. By the second week, she was really restless, for she didn't seem to be getting any better. By the third week she was sure she was never going to get better. The doctors were non-committal when she asked them, desperately, when she would be able to work—or if, for that matter, she would ever again be able to *walk*.

"Arthritis is a very stubborn disease," was all they would say. "You are, of course, unlucky to have it at your age."

The end of the first month found her utterly discouraged. To be so young and to be crippled! She lay in bed with the tears trickling down her cheeks.

This time no one helped her but herself—and possibly William Vaughn Moody. She never knew exactly when the turning point came. There was a day when snatches of the poem kept going through her head.

> *Of loss and doubt and dread,*
> *And swift oncoming doom*
> *I made a helmet for my head,*
> *And a floating plume.*

Some lines of the poem she couldn't remember, and that was tiresome. "I wish you'd look in my suitcase," she said to a young probationer who came into the room. "There's a small brown book that I want awfully. I think it is where you can see it."

The probationer found the book without difficulty. Janet turned the pages, looking for the poem. It was the book in which she had kept the poems and bits of verses that she had used for roll-call in Professor Kern's class.

"Here it is!" There was so much pleasure in her voice that the probationer was startled. Janet read the poem over. "And there's another one I like, right on the next page," she said. "It might have been written for me."

She read it aloud:

> *"For when the heavy body has grown weak,*
> *There's nothing that can tether the wild mind,*
> *That being moonstruck and fantastical,*
> *Goes where it pleases."*

Then she laughed, a laugh that was rusty from disuse. "I copied that when I was in the infirmary with measles! An Irish poet wrote it; his name was Yeats. My mind isn't exactly 'moonstruck and fantastical,' but it *can* go where it pleases!"

The probationer, a stolid Pennsylvania Dutch girl, saw nothing to laugh at. "She's queer," she said to herself. "Lies here looking grouchy all day, and then finds a silly poem and starts laughing at it." She hurried over to the window and pulled up the shade with a jerk, pulled it up too far, so that the sun shone into Janet's eyes. Then, with a rustle of her blue-and-white dress, the probationer went out of the room.

"Number 29 is talking queer," she said to the head nurse. "She says her mind can go where it pleases. And something about being moonstruck. Maybe you'd better go in and take a look at her."

"I've other things to do," said the head nurse. "Number 29 is all right. Just reads too much."

In her room, Janet lay shading her eyes from the sun, staring at the opposite wall. How foolish of her to think that she had to look at those drab walls all day! Her mind could go where it pleased. It wasn't pacing up and down, now, like a prisoner in a narrow cell. It was free! It travelled back to Trinidad and the day when she had written her own funny little poem. From there it went to Christmas day and the silver pencil shining on the tree. The picture was so clear that she felt she could reach out her hand to take the pencil. It was there on the branch between a silver trumpet and a rosy, waxen angel. . . . She made herself come back to reality. Where was the pencil now? On the table by her bed lay the writing-case that she had used as a child. Mother had mailed it to her because, she said, it would be light and easy to handle now that she was in bed.

Janet reached over for the case, opened it, ran her fingers through the pockets. She had used this writing-case when she was in England, perhaps the silver pencil. . . . Yes, there it was, in a corner of one of the pockets! She took it out eagerly. The pencil was tarnished, it was almost black, but the sunlight from the window still caught a faint gleam of silver.

Idly, she began scribbling on her writing pad. Perhaps she could write? But what? Thinking about it took her mind off the pain, for the first time in a month she began to have a real interest.

The nurses noticed the difference. Frances, prettiest and gayest of the student-nurses, put it into words.

"I don't know what has happened to you," she said. "I used to hate to come into this room, you were so sad and gloomy. Now here you are smiling and joking with us—yet I can't see you are any better. What *has* happened?"

"I don't exactly know," Janet said truthfully. "You look tired tonight. What is it?"

Frances shook the thermometer, put it in Janet's mouth, sat down by the bed. "I've had a terrible day," she said. "I don't know what made me forget, but I left a mustard-plaster too long on a patient's chest. Burned the skin off him. Almost got fired."

Janet chuckled as best she could with the thermometer in her mouth. "Don't do anything like that to me! But tell me all the things you do to other people!" It was the first time she had thought of the nurses in terms of anything but bed-making and alcohol rubs. Now they became people, with ups and downs of their own. Before long they were telling her about themselves, telling her small amusing things about the other patients.

Time went a little faster. To make it pass even more quickly, Janet took to making up verses—funny ones—about her nurses, about hospital life in general. She wrote them with the silver pencil—just for the sake of sentiment and because it was easier to use than a pen.

"Why on earth don't you do something with those verses?" asked a student-nurse called Marty.

"What *could* I do with them?" Janet wondered.

"I don't know." Marty was thoughtful. "But it seems as if there would be lots of people here who would enjoy them. Write them down, anyway."

That was how the *Hospital News* started. It was a little hard to produce, as Janet was lying almost flat, but she managed it somehow, rather slowly as the joints of her fingers were still swollen. The *Hospital News* was printed by hand on sheets of writing-paper, illustrated, too, with crude cartoon-like drawings. In prose and verse and picture, the little paper poked friendly fun at doctors and nurses, at operations and hospital diet. It circulated among the internes and nurses and went to all the patients on that floor. It came back to its editor literally worn to pieces.

And, for Janet, the hospital began to come to life. Each day brought pleasant surprises. Flowers on her breakfast tray. "From the patient in 22," Frances told her. "She liked your verse about the tonsilectomy, because she's going to have one to-morrow."

"Here are some magazines from 25," Marty said, bringing them in. "And the funny old man in 28 says will you write a poem about hardening of the arteries?"

"Mercy!" said Janet. "What next?" The friendly exchanges kept on, with all kinds of suggestions, practical and impractical, with more patients sharing their books and flowers in return for the little paper.

The days were not so long any more, nor the pain so bad. It

actually was letting up a little. Perhaps, Janet thought, when I am better I shall be able to write stories again. I feel almost as if I could."

One morning, Frances came in with a wheel chair. "You're going riding!" Her voice was cheerful.

"In that thing?" Janet looked at the chair with distaste. "I shall feel like an old, old lady."

But the chair brought a certain amount of freedom. One afternoon she wheeled it down the corridor and out onto the porch, no one had told her she could go out there, but she was going. And when she got out on the porch it was Spring. The trees were so green that they startled her. She wheeled the chair to the railing and looked down. Yellow and white crocuses starred the grass. Over in the corner the daffodils had fat green-yellow buds. A robin, his red breast bursting with prosperity, tugged hard at a worm. It really was Spring—and in a short time they would let her try to walk.

Before long she *did* walk, with slow, unsteady steps. Now the time was coming when she would have to leave the hospital, and she was actually regretful. It had come to be such a safe, friendly little world.

Frances and Marty were on another floor now, but they came back to visit. "What are you going to do when you leave us?" Frances asked. "You haven't any family in this country, have you? And you won't be able to stand on your feet long enough to teach—at least not for a while."

"I'm planning to go back to college and finish the work for my degree," Janet said. "My brother was married some months ago, but he writes that he can still help me financially. What I *don't* know is where to go this summer. Have you a suggestion?"

"I know just the place for you," Marty said eagerly. "I stayed there last summer. It's a farm, a real farm, in a little village in Nova Scotia. You'd love it, and it isn't expensive. The name of the village is Sandy Cove."

"Sandy Cove." The name had a pleasant sound as Janet said it over. "Canada is so far away," she said doubtfully.

"But worth it when you get there," Marty insisted. "Think about it, anyway. I'll give you the address."

Chapter
29

SANDY COVE

THE BUS came down the steep hill on a golden June afternoon, and Janet had her first glimpse of the village. It was not like any place she had seen before, unless it was the toy village that she had so often taken carefully out of its box when she was a little girl. White houses and churches clustered on the hill, more white houses marching down to the water's edge. Fir trees marching up toward the sky. The little Cove with its tight circle of blue water sparkling in the sunlight.

"That's David," said the bus driver, pointing out a friendly hill that rose above the village. "And Shubal," he added, pointing to a frowning hill on the other side. The bus left the village and went up the steep road that led to the Bay of Fundy. Sandy Cove, so Marty had said, was on a strip of land between two bays, with the farmhouse on the Fundy side. It was all Janet had hoped for, a long, low, homelike farm, snuggled into the hillside a little below the crest for protection from winter storms. As the bus rolled up, big quiet-eyed oxen looked at it with mild curiosity, ducks quacked and waddled frantically out of the way.

"Well, here you are!" Mrs. Ellwood, the farmer's wife, was hearty and welcoming. "You wrote me you hadn't been too well, so you must be tired. I'll take you right up to your room and you can have a good rest before dinner."

The one window of the room looked up into the stern face of Shubal. Far off, there was the sound of waves breaking on a rocky shore. Janet's body was glad to rest, her mind was busy going over the things she had seen, taking little excursions over the hill in search of the sea.

In the morning she couldn't wait any longer. She *had* to get to the top of that hill. Her legs walked slowly and stiffly up the slope, her thoughts raced on ahead of her, looked at Fundy, raced back and told her what they had seen. How tiresome! Was her mind always to race ahead like that while her body followed like a snail? When she stood on the bluff looking down on the crescent of sand, with the powerful waves rolling in, she knew that her mind hadn't been particularly reliable in its reporting. It was so much more beautiful than she had imagined. And there was something she had not been able to picture —the blue of harebells against the blue of sea and sky.

"It's a blue Nova Scotia morning, isn't it?" The voice surprised her. It belonged to a slender white-haired woman whose hands were full of harebells.

"Lovelier than anything I've seen—except perhaps some parts of Cornwall." This must be Miss Ellwood, the farmer's sister. Janet had already been told by guests at the farm that the farmer's two sisters lived in the house at the top of the hill.

"It reminds every one of some favorite spot," Miss Ellwood said. "A Frenchman told me it made him think of the Mediterranean, because the sea is so intensely blue." She smiled at Janet. "You have been ill, my brother's wife tells me. Would you like to come in and sit awhile? My sister can't get out of the house, and she loves to have visitors."

"You are very kind," Janet said. "And I'd like to sit down. Walking still makes me very tired."

They went into the house. By the living-room window sat an elderly woman who looked up welcomingly as they came in. Before she had sat in that room for five minutes, Janet knew that she was having an object lesson. For Mrs. Harvey was crippled by arthritis, could not move from her chair without assistance. It didn't matter, Janet decided, it didn't matter that her body moved so slowly and that her mind outran it. At least she could walk—*she could walk*! There was no need to feel rebellious, only a great need to feel thankful.

"I like to sit here by the window," Mrs. Harvey said. "Because then I can see Letty's garden—and a garden is lots of company."

They sat and talked for a long time. "Come back often," Miss Ellwood said when Janet left.

Each day it was easier to get up the hill, and after a while Janet walked triumphantly all the way down to the village. She was beginning to find out how different and how interesting this village was. For the first time she was really sure that she could write a book. Everything, it seemed, had its compensations. If illness had not come, perhaps she would never have slowed down long enough to write. Perhaps she would have been too preoccupied with her teaching. At all events, here she was, and here was the time and—she was certain—the story material.

Yes, stories were right at hand, she didn't have to go far to look for them. Out by the barn, a white kitten and its mother strolled across the yard. "We always have white kittens around," Mr. Ellwood said. "Once we had *seven* white cats."

Seven white cats! That was the title for a story. She would have to find out more about those cats, to let her imagination do the rest. A village boy came down the road from Fundy, proudly swinging a big fish. It had been his first deep-sea fishing trip, and he was still greenly, desperately seasick—but he wasn't letting on. Another story! So they grew, and began, in Janet's mind, to take definite form.

Somewhere she had read that any one who wanted to write should keep a notebook in which plots, outlines, details of stories were written down. Perhaps some people could do it that way, she wasn't systematic enough, didn't think she wanted to be. She kept her stories in her head, where they had room to grow; she kept fitting together the bits that came to her as she talked with the village people. She watched her friend, Miss Ellwood, searching in her bag for patchwork pieces to fit the quilt she was making.

"Story-writing is like patchwork," Janet said. "There are so many pieces to be selected from, and whether the story is good or not depends on the way one fits them together."

"And on the stitching!" Miss Letty's eyes twinkled. "And on the quilting! If you are as careful in the way you make your stories as we are in the way we make our quilts, they should have good workmanship."

"I'll try," Janet said. "But I'm a beginner, and you have been making quilts for years."

"My first one wasn't so bad," Miss Letty said meditatively. "Being a beginner isn't any excuse for sloppy work. At least that's what my mother used to tell me."

Now the stories were asking to be written down. Janet wrote sitting on the rocks, among the flowers in Miss Letty's garden, in the meadow where the salt wind rippled through the grass, making the harebells dance on their slender stems. She drew funny little pictures of cats and children, fish and fir trees, that might or might not be of assistance to the artist who would make the illustrations, and she wondered at herself for taking for granted that the stories would be in a book. If they never found themselves between covers she would still have had the fun of writing them. That was what mattered most.

The other thing that mattered was that her friends in the hilltop house were so interested in the stories. They kept adding local color, making suggestions.

"Yes, you can call your children Abigail and Sara—those are good old Nova Scotia names, just as they are good New England names."

"Your flowers aren't quite right. They bloom at odd seasons here. You can put goldenrod and wild roses right on the same page."

"Tell some of the names of the patchwork quilts—Roundabout — Wedding Ring — Schoolhouse — they have a good sound."

So it went, in the friendliest sort of way. Janet began to feel that the stories were as much theirs as hers. When, at the end of the summer, the bus took her away from Sandy Cove, her suitcase was full of closely written yellow sheets. But the stories had no title. She must think of one on the way back, or at least sometime before she took the manuscript to a publisher.

Chapter 30

FINDING A PUBLISHER

THE BOOK and its title were temporarily forgotten when Janet got back to New York. For Mary was there; they were going to have rooms in the same house, and Mary would take postgraduate work at Columbia. Most important of all, she brought firsthand news of Janet's family. It seemed as if they would never get through talking. Janet was full of eager questions—mostly about the baby nephew who had arrived just before Mary left Trinidad.

"Does Mother look any older? Is Lawrence as much fun, or has he settled down since he was married? Is the baby cute? Lawrence writes that he has dark hair and eyes—I did hope he'd be blond like our side of the family. Is Bea as silly as ever? What does she think of the baby?"

Mary answered the questions to the best of her ability and then began to ask some of her own.

"What have you been doing since you left the hospital, Jan?" Did you get started on a book? You wrote that you wanted to."

"I got started and I finished it," Janet said. "But I don't know whether it's any good or not. I'd like you to read it. Do you happen to know what one does about sending—or taking—a book to a publisher? I haven't the least idea how to go about it."

"Nor I," said Mary. "I'm glad you finished the book, but the thing that pleases me most is that you can *walk*. We must have some fun this year. I think we'd better start with that party at the International Club this week. You can't dance, of course, but this isn't a dance, it's a sort of costume party. We must think up some costumes."

"Fun! It seems ages since I had any fun of that kind. And I have an idea about costumes. It isn't original—I saw it in a book. We could go as date palms."

"Date palms? How on earth?"

"Simple enough. Burlap. Wire. Green paper. Honest-to-goodness dates. It's rather a trick idea because every one says: 'May I have a date?' "

"Well—" Mary was still dubious. "If you think it will work out . . ."

"Of course it will. Now tell me some more about the baby. Did you really hold him?"

On the night of the party the girls arrived together and were instantly a success. They were wound tightly in strips of burlap, with holes cut for their arms and for their faces. Above their heads waved luxuriant paper fronds from which dangled real dates. It was amusing to have every one come up and say, "May I have a date?" At least it was amusing up to about the twentieth time, then it began to wear a little thin. And about that time their feet began to hurt.

"Janet"—there was real anguish in Mary's voice—"I knew when you planned this costume that we weren't going to be able to sit down. But I didn't want to say anything, you seemed so set on it."

"I know!" Janet was regretful. "But we are sure to win the prize."

"Just what will *that* do for us? We aren't going to be able to do anything all evening. Just stand and talk about dates."

"May I have a date?" The voice was familiar. The owner of it wore a pair of pajamas, a towel draped around him, another on his head, and many assorted sponges.

"Hank! What are you doing at Columbia? Mary, you know about Hank? And what is your costume supposed to be?"

"I'm here to take some work in chemistry—don't want to stay in one place all my life. And I'm the Knight of the Bath. Silly, but a good deal more comfortable than your costume!"

"It wouldn't have to go far to be! They're starting the Grand March and after that they'll award the prizes. If we win I won't care how much our feet hurt."

The date palms won the prize, but it wasn't much of a consolation. Janet knew by now that she was not going to be able to stand on her feet much longer. Why had she been so foolish?

"I'll leave any time you want to," Mary said. "My feet are getting used to it, but I know how it must be about yours."

"I think I'll try leaning a while," Janet said. She went over into a corner and leaned wearily against the wall. It didn't help. She shifted her weight from one foot to the other.

"Whatever is the matter, Jan? I've been watching you for the last five minutes and you look perfectly miserable." It was Hank again.

"Oh, Hank, will you take me home? I don't want Mary to leave, she seems to be having a good time. But my feet hurt terribly."

"I'll be glad to. It's a good thing I have my car here—I don't believe you could walk a block. And I used to think you had some sense!"

It was a great relief to be taken home, and it was fun to be with Hank again. But the car presented difficulties. Janet couldn't get in and so she simply stood and looked at it.

"Holy smoke! What are we going to do? I guess you'll have to ride on the running board. And if I get arrested for driving around the campus with a date palm on the running board, you can bail me out!"

They drove slowly to the street where Janet lived. "Hank," she said as they went up Broadway. "Do you know anything about publishers?"

"Lord, no," said Hank. "Should I?"

"I just wondered. You see I've written a book for children and I don't know just what to do with it."

"Sorry I can't help you out. I should think the thing to do would be to choose your publisher and then take your book there. Or send it. I don't think it really matters, if it's a good book it will make its own way."

"It sounds so easy," Janet said. "Only I can't decide on the publisher! Here's my house. Thanks awfully, Hank." She stepped stiffly from the running board, just as the policeman on the beat came along, but he did not give her so much as a glance. Around the college campus a policeman got used to seeing unusual things.

"Good night," said Hank. "Don't go so literary you can't go to a movie once in a while! I'm counting on you, Jan."

The question of a publisher was, after all, settled very simply. Janet looked over the children's books in the library and decided that those published by the Mansfield Company appealed to her. So, on a chilly November day, she and her manuscript boarded a Fifth Avenue bus. Down the magnificent sweep of Riverside Drive, through crowded streets, and at last they were on Fifth Avenue. And as the numbers on the numbered cross-streets began to grow smaller, the manuscript, never very large, seemed to shrink. As the bus passed the big Public Library, the manuscript was only half its size and the Library lions seemed to smile with amused tolerance. At the Flatiron Building the manuscript shrank into nothingness. It was such a little thing, why had she ever thought it was important enough to take to a publisher? If she stayed on the bus it would eventually turn around and take her home. But she had an appointment with the editor and she must see it through. So, on lower Fifth Avenue, she got off the bus.

The publishing house was alarmingly square and solid. Janet drew a long breath and went in. If the manuscript had not already seemed to vanish, it would surely have done so during the minutes she sat in the waiting room. She looked down at it as it lay in her lap. What a slim little thing it was! And it had no title. Hastily taking out her pen, she wrote on the blank first page: *Salt Water Stories*. It was a simple solution, why hadn't she thought of it before?

"Miss Marshall will see you." The editor's secretary came out to make this announcement. She looked at Janet without curiosity; it was evident that would-be authors were far from exciting to her. Janet followed the secretary through an avenue of clicking typewriters to the Editor's office. It was a pleasant room with shelves of colorful books. The Editor was in the middle of a telephone conversation, her voice brisk and competent. She was telling a printer, politely but in picturesque language, exactly what she thought of a job he had done for her. She motioned to Janet to sit down. Then she turned from the telephone and Janet found herself looking into a pair of the keenest blue eyes she had ever seen. They smiled at her, crinkling up at the corners, while the Editor's mouth remained disciplined and scarcely smiled at all. Miss Marshall, Janet noted with relief, wasn't any older than she was.

"Tell me about your book, Miss Laidlaw?" The voice was quite different from that of the telephone conversation. There was so much warmth in it that the manuscript was immediately restored to its proper size, even began to take on some importance. And why not? It had now ceased to be a manuscript, it was a *book*!

"It is something that I wrote when I was in a little fishing village in Nova Scotia." Janet was amazed at the confidence in her voice. "I think the setting is unusual."

The Editor held out her hand for the manuscript. "I like your title," she said. "The village sounds fascinating. I'd love to know something about it." And Janet, now perfectly at ease, told about the Cove and its people, about the farm and the oxen, about her friends in the hill-top house.

"Miss Brooks is here." The secretary's voice broke in on Janet's story.

"Goodness!" the Editor said. "I promised to lunch with her. I'd no idea it was so late! Ask her to wait just a minute, will you? Miss Laidlaw, if you'll leave your book I'll read it and write you about it. By the way, that is Margaret Brooks. I think you may know her poems."

On the way out Janet had a brief glimpse of Margaret Brooks. Know her poems! Of course she did. Margaret Brooks was one of the best known writers in the children's field. To think that she—Janet—might have her book on the same publisher's list! Some day she might even meet Margaret Brooks. Then she could tell her how she loved her poems, especially the one about the fir trees.

The bus seemed to gallop up Fifth Avenue. The Library lions still wore their peculiar, remote smile. "Don't count your chickens before they are hatched," they seemed to say. But Janet was not in any mood to be discouraged. Something told her that the Editor would like her stories. Of course she might *like* them, but not enough to *publish* them. One could only wait and see.

It was hard to wait. Every day, when she went down to the mailbox, Janet expected to see a letter from the Mansfield Company. But none came. One week, two, three. Should she call them up? Perhaps the Editor had put the manuscript away and had forgotten it. No, she wasn't the kind of person who would forget. And even if she did, that very businesslike secretary would be on the job. Janet decided to be patient.

And then the letter came. Janet almost stopped breathing as she took it out of the mailbox. It was very slim, but that didn't mean anything. Probably they were returning her manuscript "under separate cover." She wanted to open the letter and she didn't want to. It was Saturday morning and Mary would still be in her room; if the letter should turn out to be a rejection it would be necessary to have some one to sympathize. So, still with the letter unopened, she took the elevator up to Mary's floor.

"The letter from the Mansfield Company?" Mary's voice held the excitement that Janet felt. "Sit down and open it. No, here on the couch so I can see, too." They sat down and Janet opened the envelope. Her hands shook a little as she unfolded the sheet of paper. The words danced before her eyes: "Like your stories . . . charming . . . wish to publish . . . come down and talk it over . . ."

"Gosh!" said Mary. "They've taken it!" Janet said nothing. She couldn't.

"Do you know how lucky you are, Jan? To get a book accepted by the first publisher you took it to? Do you?"

"Yes," Janet said. "I do know." She went to the window and stood looking out. She and Margaret Brooks on the same list! She couldn't believe it. Then she thought: *If only I could tell Father about it. He was always so proud of my stories!*

Chapter 31 *ACROSS THE RIVER*

THE NEXT DAY the bus took Janet down Fifth Avenue again but this time everything was different.

Yes, she thought as she passed the Library lions. You will soon be guarding my book among all the others. But would they? Books for the Children's Room were carefully selected, she knew that. Perhaps hers wouldn't make the grade. Perhaps she shouldn't even expect a first book to be admitted. There she went, crossing bridges again! She thought she'd broken herself of that habit but here it was popping up once more.

When she talked with Jane Marshall about the book, Janet was again full of confidence. Jane Marshall had a gift for making each author feel that "the book" was the only one in the world. There were other books on the list of course, but it was *this* one that counted. They talked of illustrations. "I know just the artist for you," Jane Marshall said. "She can draw children who look like real children, and that is what we must have for your stories."

The weeks that followed were full of bliss. Like almost all authors of a first book, Janet was surprised that it took so long to get her child between covers. She had thought that it was a matter of a month or so, but her book would not be published until quite late in the spring. "And even that is quick work," Jane Marshall told her. "Usually it takes a year or more." Each month held its own particular magic. There was the magic of galley proof—those long, shiny proofs that were so awkward to read and from which one's words looked up at one set so finally in type. Oh, not too finally, for there could be changes in galleys—though very few, the publishers told her sternly, in page proof. There was the magic of page proof—and the magic of pictures. Of course no artist could quite see eye to eye with the author. The children were not really her children, they belonged to the artist, but that was only what one had to expect. That little dark-haired boy, for example, she never in this world could have thought *him* up. He wasn't just the way she wanted him, but she would be pleasant and forbearing and she would adopt him.

That was how she felt about Lawrence's baby. He didn't look in the least like the family, but she had adopted him. Lawrence was so proud, and pictures of the baby came in every letter. He and the book seemed to grow together, with illustrations and a first tooth arriving at almost the same moment.

Mother wrote glowingly of the new addition to the family. She was thoroughly enjoying being a grandmother—and for the first time her letters were not full of detail as to how she missed her daughter. "I hope it won't be long before you have a home and babies of your own," she wrote. "There's nothing like them. A book is fine, of course, and we are proud of you. But I want you to marry and have a family."

It all made Janet a trifle lonesome, for, after all, a furnished room was no substitute for a home. She began to feel a little more kindly towards Hank. He had, of course, been surprisingly casual about her book, but then he was intelligent and perhaps she shouldn't expect him to get excited about a book for children. He was rather solid, not overgifted with imagination, at least not with her kind of imagination. But he would undoubtedly make a good husband. She had spent the last few weeks warding off a proposal, for Hank was the kind who had to put everything neatly and finally into words, to tie all ends firmly and leave nothing to supposition. Janet could always see the proposal coming, it was as if he had taken it out of his pocket and spread it out on his knees, ready for use. He never got a chance to use it, however, and always it was neatly folded and put back into his pocket, waiting for a more suitable time. Janet was really surprised that Hank cared anything at all about her, apparently he had quite forgotten the pact that they had made when they first met.

On the afternoon when her mother's letter came, Janet, in a softened mood, went with Hank to the Palisades, across the river. He liked to walk, and she could walk fairly well now. Hank always saw to it that she did not walk too far.

They crossed on the ferry, Hank talking, as he so often did, mainly about himself. Janet managed, with some difficulty, to get in a few fragments about the baby nephew, for she was spilling over with pride. But the wind caught the words and tossed them into the river—at least so it seemed, for Hank kept on talking steadily about his after-college plans. He was going to teach in a town not far from New York.

"It's a good place to work," he said. "And," looking at Janet, "a nice place to live."

Janet returned, hastily, to the subject of the baby nephew, for she felt Hank was beginning to polish up the proposal, preparatory to taking it out. But she understood, all at once, that he wasn't only talking about himself, that he took it for granted she was included in his plans. Good old Hank, he wasn't a bit thrilling, but, after all— She moved over a little nearer to him and put her hand on his arm. He had been a friend when she needed one.

When they reached the Palisades they walked for a short time, then sat on a little hill, looking over the river. It was late April and the trees wore their new green leaves with pride. There were small star-like flowers in the grass. Janet idly picked one and put it in Hank's buttonhole. "No trillium here," she said. "This will have to do instead."

That was a mistake. She could see him taking out the proposal now, spreading it, getting all the corners neatly in place. If he had simply leaned over and kissed her, everything might have been all right. But he was so careful, so slow in his approach that, mentally, she had time to build a high fence around herself. That was the trouble, he was so deliberate in his thinking that she was always two jumps ahead of him.

Quite unconscious of all this, Hank followed his own line.

"I was there the other day," he said, "and I looked the ground over pretty thoroughly."

"Yes?" Janet felt she might as well be a little encouraging and help him along.

"I looked the ground over and it seemed like a nice little town. Up on the hill near the college there were some houses that looked pretty good to me." A faraway expression came into Hank's eyes. "I thought that a girl might like them. She could keep house there so easily—you should see the kitchen— and she wouldn't have to do anything else——"

Wouldn't have to do anything else! Janet knew now that Hank really didn't care about her writing. She wondered what she would say. At that moment a most disreputable old tramp, ragged, unwashed, unshaven, came down the hill and seated himself a few feet away. He fixed his eyes on them, grinned knowingly.

"Keep right on with your talk, kids," he said. "Don't mind me. I was young myself, once."

"I think we had better be getting home," said Janet hastily. "I don't think—somehow that I am especially interested in houses. I'm not a bit domestic."

"That's the girl," chortled the tramp. "Keep 'em guessing!"

"Come on!" Hank's voice was savage. This time the tattered proposal couldn't even be folded, it had to be rudely hustled back into place. They got up and walked toward the ferry.

On the way home they stood at the bow of the boat, saying nothing at all. But Janet felt that the next time Hank took out the proposal it would be for another girl. Perhaps she had hurt him; she was sorry if she had, but there was an ache in it for her, too. For there was no use pretending to herself, no way of getting around it—she would have lived in any of those little houses with Stephen.

Chapter
32 "SALT WATER STORIES"

THE TELEPHONE rang in the hall outside of Janet's room and she answered it. At the other end was the voice that she had come to associate with all kinds of pleasant and thrilling experiences. "Do you suppose you can come down today?" Jane Marshall said. "I have an advance copy of your book. Of course I could mail it, but it would be ever so much nicer if you could come."

Ever so much nicer! Janet could hardly get there soon enough. The bus seemed to take hours to make the trip; the few minutes that she waited in the reception room were endless. Today when the secretary came to summon her, the girl was positively beaming. "We all think your book looks lovely," she told Janet. "We hope you'll think so, too."

Through the avenue of typewriters again, and into Jane Marshall's office. Jane—they were using first names now, for that comes very quickly in the publishing business—was waiting for her, the book on her desk. Janet saw the cheerful colors of the jacket, the title—her own name leaped out at her in letters that seemed simply enormous.

"Here it is, at last." Jane smiled with her eyes as she handed the book to Janet. "I do hope you'll like it."

The feel of the book in her hands was thrilling. The smell of print was intoxicating. Janet opened the book to the story of the fisher boy. The words looked entirely unfamiliar, had she really written them?

"Well?" Jane cocked an eyebrow in a familiar, inquiring gesture. "Do you, or don't you?"

"Of course I do. It looks simply wonderful. I just can't get used to the thought that it's mine."

Jane laughed. "I like to see an author get the first glimpse of her book. You can see why I don't usually send them by mail. Of course not all of them like the book. Sometimes they fuss. But usually they fuss about the second book and the third—and get fussier from then on. The first one usually goes over well!"

"I'll never fuss about any of them."

"Don't you believe it! But something tells me you won't be the kind who haunts bookstores and is always calling up and complaining that the book isn't to be found in this store or that. Margaret Brooks isn't that kind, either. By the way, she's coming in to return her proofs and I think you two should meet. You seem to like many of the same things."

They not only met, but they went out of the office together. Margaret Brooks was a tall girl with red-brown hair and a serious expression, but, so Janet discovered in a very short time, a grand sense of humor. They walked up the Avenue to Fourteenth Street.

"Jane has told me about your book," Margaret said. "Sandy Cove sounds like a place I want to see. It isn't so very different from Maine, where I go in the summer."

"No," said Janet. "I thought when I first read your poems

that they were about Nova Scotia. I'd give anything in the world to write poems like yours. But I never shall."

"You do your own kind of writing," said Margaret. "And Jane thinks your book is good. We're lucky to have her for an editor, she's the kind who brings out the best you have in you. I have to take the crosstown car, I'm going to see a friend in Chelsea. But I wish you'd come to tea some day next week. We have lots to talk about. I'll call you up."

All the way home on the bus the book was warm under Janet's fingers. But the pleasure of it was mixed with the pleasure of meeting Margaret. They were going to be friends, of that she was sure. In the few months that had gone into the making of her book she had made two friends—even though one friendship was just beginning. Books were going to bring her many new friendships, many interesting contacts. It was like going into an entirely new world. Strange, she thought, how friends come when you need them most! Some of them come and stay a long time, like Mary and Helen, others come in and go out, but always leave something of themselves. Thinking of friends—Mary must be the next person to see the book. The days were warm now and Mary, who hated to be indoors, would probably be somewhere on the campus. Janet decided to try to find her.

The grass of the campus was fresh and green, the irises were in bloom. The squirrels were out, looking hopefully for peanuts. It seemed to Janet that they took a minute or two off from food-hunting to look at her and to jerk their tails in congratulation. "So you've written a book," with quick jerks of the tail. "So—you've—written—a—book." Janet laughed at herself as she thought it. Why, here she was getting to be what Jane called "authory"! It would never do. But maybe, just for one day, one could be awfully pleased and proud.

There seemed to be a great many trees on the campus, but at last she found Mary, sitting with her back against a maple. Janet came up behind her, quietly, and dropped the book in her lap.

"Heavens!" said Mary. "How you startled me!" She picked up the book. "Oh, Jan, it looks simply handsome. Aren't you pleased?"

"Thrilled," said Janet, sitting down beside her. "Only I still have a queer impersonal feeling about it—as if some one else had written it. Mary—if it hadn't been for you this book wouldn't be here. You are the one who gave me courage to come to America."

Chapter
33
WESTWARD

IT SEEMED impossible that two such wonderful things could happen in one year—the book—and the promise of the most important position Janet had held as yet, one that frightened while it thrilled her because it *was* so important. She was to return to Teachers College in the fall and to be one of three assistants to the director of the big demonstration kindergarten.

And in June came Commencement.

"I'd never have believed it," Janet said as Mary helped to straighten the white collar on her gown. "But here I am, getting a college degree, after all, and I'll be as proud of my blue-and-white Columbia hood as I would have been of the English one —perhaps even prouder."

Mary laughed. "Put the tassel of your cap over on the other side. There—you look wonderful. After all, your mother did the right thing when she didn't let you go to Girton, though she couldn't possibly have known it at the time. It's really better for you to have a degree in education than just a plain B.A."

"I wish she and Lawrence could be here today," Janet said.

"I'll send them a snap of you in your cap and gown. Come outside and let me take it. I promised Hank——"

"Oh, *Hank*," said Janet. "*Hank*." Her voice curled scornfully around the name. "He won't want it now."

"Why can't you be nicer to him?" Mary asked.

"If you must know—because Stephen still gets in the way. And also because I don't happen to love Hank."

"H'm. I thought as much." Mary looked regretful. "Come on, let's get the picture taken, it's almost time for you to go over to college."

It was very much a mass Commencement, with the many hundreds of students graduating from the big university, but although there was no individual presentation of diplomas, the graduating exercises were thrilling in their very vastness. Janet happened to be with the group of undergraduates who, because of lack of space in the body of the hall, sat on the platform with the faculty. *How dull black gowns are*, she thought. *If only we could wear red!* For the one brilliant spot of color was the scarlet gown worn by the president of the University, a gown that he had acquired in Europe. Near the president sat the candidates for honorary degrees.

"Look!" Janet whispered to the girl who sat next to her

"There's Paderewski! Isn't his hair marvellous? Wouldn't he be stunning in Nick's red gown?" Nick was what the students called the President.

"Shh! Things are beginning."

As the Commencement exercises progressed, degrees were awarded by classes. Janet rose with her group, listened politely, sat down again wearing the aura of a degree. At last came the dramatic moment when the graduates of the School of Medicine rose to take the Hippocratic Oath. The Dean of the School of Medicine read the words, the young doctors raised their hands . . .

Stephen! Stephen! Stephen! The name rushed at Janet with such force that she was convinced some one had said it aloud. For the young doctor at the end of the second row, hand upraised, eyes fixed on the Dean, was Stephen. The School of Medicine was in a different part of the city, so Janet had not seen any of the medical students. She had not tried to find out what Stephen was doing, had deliberately put him out of her mind. And now, here he was.

The students of the Medical School sat down. The President rose to award the honorary degrees. To Janet everything was a blur until the name came that called her back to attention—"Ignace Jan Paderewski." I must remember this, Janet said to herself with fierce determination. "It is a Great Moment and I must remember it and write home about it." But, in spite of herself, pieces of the Great Moment slipped away, she hardly saw the President as he placed the Columbia hood on the famous musician. Then the band broke into Paderewski's *Minuet* and the students rose in tribute. Janet looked down at the Medical School and Stephen's eyes met hers. He smiled, a wavering smile; Janet never knew if she had smiled back. But she saw no more of Paderewski, of the President and his scarlet gown, and she scarcely knew when the exercises were over.

Stephen waited for her at the campus gate. "Hi, there!" he said as casually as if he had seen her only yesterday.

"Hello, Stephen," Janet hoped her voice was as steady and as casual as his. "I didn't know you were graduating this year."

"I'm a year late," said Stephen. "The war held me up. I was in the army but I never got over to France."

Janet felt around in her mind for something to say, then said the one thing she least wanted to, said it abruptly and awkwardly. "How's Lily?"

Stephen's eyes had a faraway look as if he were searching into his past trying to disentangle Lily from many others. "Lily? I guess she's well enough. Seems to me I heard she was married . . ."

It was important to say something else and to say it quickly. Janet hurried into "How's George?" That seemed safe.

But it wasn't. Stephen grinned, that slow, remembered grin, his eyes lighting up. "George is fine. He's all ready to go to work with me. What about having dinner with me some night this week, to talk about—George?" His voice was as teasing, as caressing as ever.

"No, you don't," Janet said to herself. "Don't let it get you again." She felt as if she were being torn in two. Aloud she said, her voice cool and steady, "Thank you, Stephen, but I'm afraid I'm too busy. You see I'm going to teach in North Dakota this summer and I have to get ready to go. I'm sorry I won't be able to talk about—George."

Stephen looked at her unbelievingly. "Oh, well, if that's the way you want it," he said and, turning, went off across the campus.

An hour later, Mary found Janet packing with a fierceness that seemed uncalled for.

"How does it seem to have a B.S.? . . . Janet! Whatever is the matter?"

"Nothing." Janet tried to sound casual. "I saw Stephen."

"Stephen? What was he doing there?"

"Getting his degree. He's a medical student, you know."

"For heaven's sake! You aren't going to see him again?"

"No. I'm not."

"Are you sure?"

"Perfectly sure. I seem to have outgrown Stephen. I began to feel that the moment he spoke to me."

"But all the same it's just as well you are going to North Dakota!"

And Janet was glad, too, when she found herself on the train, that there would be miles between her and New York that summer. She was going with confidence to the position that had offered itself—to teach kindergarten-primary work in a normal school. She had not taught theory in a normal school before, but what of it?

"Teaching is an elastic profession." Janet remembered Martha's words on that mournful day in Geneseo. Teaching was certainly taking her to many new places. Of course, she said to herself, it didn't do that for every one. Sometimes you were just set down in a little rural school and stayed there all your life. But teaching *was* like a rubber band. It could expand and take in all kinds of experience, or it could remain, wound tight and unyielding, around the small package that was your life. Perhaps it had something to do with the kind of person you were. Perhaps it only depended on circumstances. She didn't know.

"Are you going far?" asked a pleasant, very English voice from across the aisle. Janet looked across to see a girl of about her own age smiling at her.

"North Dakota. And you?"

"Nebraska. My father has a ranch there and I visit him every other summer."

"Do you live in England?"

"Yes, I teach at Girton. Have you been across?"

Girton! thought Janet. Of all places! Aloud she said, "Yes, I'm British. I went to school in England—Wimbledon Hill."

"Well!" said the girl. "So did I! Think of meeting an old Wimbledonian over here."

They exchanged names. Rose Weller had been in the sixth form while Janet was still at school. It was an amazing coincidence.

"What is North Dakota really like?" asked Rose. "I've only been through it on the train."

"I haven't an idea," Janet said. "I've only seen it on the map. It's awfully square on that. And I'm dying to see prairies. I've never seen one. The dictionary says a prairie is 'an extensive level treeless tract of land covered with coarse grass.' I hope there are trees at Valley City—that's where I'm going to teach."

"So we're both teachers," Rose said. "I always look at the schools as I travel across country and wonder how it would feel to work in them. I wonder, too, why so many towns and cities haven't more imagination when they build their schools."

Janet looked out of the window. "You can always tell the primary grade rooms," she said. "Snowflakes or tulips, or windmills or Eskimos pasted on the windows. I wonder how it feels to look out endlessly at sky and trees through Eskimos."

Rose laughed. "And even though it's June, some of the schools are still in the tulip stage—and a few haven't got beyond snowflakes."

The colored paper seasons marched with them across the country, through Ohio, Indiana, Illinois and Iowa. "After all," Janet said, "they'll know better in North Dakota—when this summer is over."

"Don't be too sure!" said Rose.

They were in the prairie state the next morning and it *was* flat—flat as the palm of one's hand. Level fields stretched into the distance with here and there a farmhouse and its windbreak of carefully nurtured trees.

What a country this must be in winter," Janet thought. A rural school swung into sudden close-up, its windows neatly patterned with snowflakes. She smiled grimly at it.

"Valley City!" shouted the conductor. "Valley City!" It would have been nice to say good-bye to Rose, but she was still asleep. Janet looked out of the window of the still-moving train. They seemed to be in the middle of a prairie and it was six o'clock in the morning. Janet felt like a very small fly about to alight on a billiard table, but the station came, eventually, and there *were* trees, lots of them.

There were taxis, too, and one took her to the house to which she had written to reserve a room. It was still very early and every one was asleep. Janet tried the door cautiously; it was open, so she walked in.

"Of course we don't lock our doors." Mrs. James was up now, sleepy-eyed but hospitable. "This is an honest town." It must be an honest town, Janet thought, her room cost so little. Why she had a bedroom and an enormous sleeping porch and when she paid for them each week it was with four of those unbelievably heavy silver cartwheels that for some reason this part of the country seemed to prefer to dollar bills.

Valley City didn't consider itself very "Far West," but to Janet it was. The small, rather bare Main Street, with every one in shirt sleeves in the heat of the day, and on Saturday nights farmers coming in to go to the pictures, and Indians coming from a nearby reservation. These were the first American Indians Janet had seen, though, to tell the truth, she had almost expected to meet them in Brooklyn. And why not? In her childhood East Indians had lived within a stone's throw of her house.

Many of the students were Scandinavian. Most of them had not been through high school, some had lived on farms throughout their lives and had limited experience. Quite a number of young men were in the class, and, to Janet's amazement, some of them were going to teach in primary grades.

From the crowd of students two soon stood out. Marybelle, because of her funny, silly name and because of her startling, empty beauty combined with the brain of a very small bird. Marybelle was all blondness and dimples and shapely legs. She had taken up teaching because she could get tuition free—so many girls went into it for that reason—and it was something to put in the time with until one married. Scarcely an idea ever got past the golden tangle that was her hair or lighted the blue vacuums that were her eyes.

The other was Mrs. Olsen, a small white-haired woman who must have been fifty-five, and who was taking a summer course to brush up on her teaching. Her clear gray eyes, set in a weathered face, were alive and eager. She came only to afternoon classes; Janet wondered why. Finally she asked her.

"Because of the threshing," Mrs. Olsen said in a matter-of-fact way. "I run the farm since my husband died. Teach school, too. This is threshing season—all the threshers to be fed. I come after I have given them their dinner."

It made Janet feel citified and ignorant. But Mrs. Olsen didn't seem to feel superior, indeed she was very friendly. One day after class they got to talking about teaching.

"It must be rather dull—limiting—to teach always in a small rural school," Janet ventured.

Mrs. Olsen's eyes were full of surprise. "Dull? Limiting? It's exactly what you make of it. I've always found it an adventure. Just the children themselves are an adventure—and so many things happen. Even from the beginning. I remember my first school. It was a very small one and I boarded with the family that made up quite a part of the school enrollment—five children. I hadn't been there a month before the woman had twins. And I had to do everything. Oh, yes—her husband went for the doctor but he didn't get there in time. Yes, I did everything. How'd I know what to do? I didn't. But she'd had five children, remember, and she told me what to do. She called one of the twins after me—they were boy and girl."

"Goodness!" Janet said. It seemed an inadequate remark, but it was all she could manage to say.

"And there was the year when I was snowed in." Mrs. Olsen was enjoying herself. "The blizzard came on so quick I didn't have time to get the children home. Luckily we had plenty of wood and when I saw how it was going to be, I told the children to save half of what was in their lunch pails. The snow came all the way up to the roof, and the children were pretty hungry before they dug us out. They took it well, though. Children in this state grow up with blizzards. My husband and I were engaged then, it was he and some of the children's fathers who dug us out. I didn't go back to teaching until my husband died—but I've always loved it." Her eyes were warm and humorous.

Marybelle, who, for some reason had been working overtime, looked up as Mrs. Olsen finished her story.

"You can have it on a silver platter," she said. "For me it's only so much a month until the right fellow comes along. I've got no patience with the kids. Nor with this stuff"—she indicated the project she was working on. It was a neat Pilgrim village, with log cabins made of corrugated cardboard and Pilgrims of clothespins. Marybelle had a way with her hands if not with her head.

Janet groaned. "But why Pilgrims? I told you all to work out your project in the history of your own state. *Sod* cabins, not *log* cabins. North Dakota pioneers, not Pilgrims."

Marybelle looked stolid. "I should go out and dig up sods," she said. "And get dirt in my finger nails, when this cardboard makes a log cabin so easy. And Pilgrims—I like the costume. Kind of cute with those big collars and white caps."

Somewhere on the prairie, Janet knew, there would be a small schoolhouse with windows snowflaked in June. But not for long. Marybelle was too pretty.

They drove out one afternoon, Janet and Mrs. Olsen, in the shaky old Ford, out onto the prairie. It was a long ride through miles and miles of golden wheat. Wheat stretching to the horizon—it wasn't possible that there was so much wheat in the world. The big reapers, four horses abreast, cutting and binding as they went, had a magnificent sweep. Janet had thought a prairie state couldn't be beautiful—for beauty, to her eyes, was rolling country, hills, mountains. But this golden land had a beauty of its own.

"I didn't know flat country could be so lovely," she said.

"It's all in the way you look at it." Mrs. Olsen's steady eyes looked out across the acres of grain with affection. "Some folks like the hills crowding in close around them and shutting out the view. Others of us like this land where nothing gets in the way and you can see clear to the horizon—north, south, east and west. Now I just can't stand it if anything gets between me and the horizon. Why, I went to visit in Vermont and I was so homesick I *cried*. Mountains standing there peering down at me. I had to come home. Nothing like mountains for making one feel lonesome."

Janet laughed. "That's an entirely new point of view to me! I suppose it's because I grew up in a little town snuggled at the foot of a hill, but its *flat* country that makes me feel lonely. When I first came here I didn't like it a bit." As they drove home she did not talk very much. This was such a *big* country, with such wide differences, one could only get to know it slowly, piece by piece. Would she, island born and raised, ever feel at home in it? Would she ever be part of it? To be an American one would have forever to think of life as painted on a broad canvas.

Chapter
34

THAT WINTER, when she was back in New York, Janet knew once and for all that she was meant to be a teacher. There was something rewarding about it, something thrilling and heart-warming. The big kindergarten room on a cold day, with logs blazing in the fireplace and children gathered around to pop corn. Children with eager faces, children to whom popping corn was nothing short of a miracle, because they lived in apart-ments without fireplaces. Christmas time—trees gay with crude, childlike paper trimmings, and tall ladders by which one stood to steady uncertain young legs. Children poring eagerly over picture books—read this one—please—oh, don't stop, just *one* more!

And the year brought Martin and Mark. Teaching was a long procession of children, some of them would come and go —be only names—dimly remembered faces. A few would stay for ever in clear shining memory, as did these two small boys, utterly different from each other.

Martin was the most beautiful child in the kindergarten. Small, alert, with curly brown hair and enormous gray eyes— perfect features and that unearthly look that one sees only once in a while in a child's face. He brimmed over with imagination, lived for the moment when he could get the children in a group to "play a story." Martin seldom took part himself, he directed —and no story was too difficult for him to attempt.

So when Christmas came, it was inevitable that, his imagination kindled by the Christmas story, he should want to put it into action. This did not surprise Janet at all, what did surprise her was that she was chosen for a part in the drama. Usually she was a helpful onlooker.

"You," said Martin, his eyes glowing with the joy of planning this beautiful thing, "are the Mother Mary. And Dickie is the Christ Child."

A wave of self-consciousness, something she had not felt for a long time, came over Janet. Students would be coming in and out, mothers would arrive, for it was near the end of the morning. How *could* she be the Mother with Dickie—golden-haired but oversize for a baby—on her lap?

Then she shook herself mentally. "Of course you're going to do it." She sat down on a low chair and gathered Dickie into her lap. Obligingly he curled himself into a ball.

"I'm a big baby," he said, looking up at her apologetically. "I'll make my legs smaller."

Martin was choosing the others. "You be the Three Wise Men; the Shepherds; you are Joseph. You are the ox—the ass. And you"—waving a hand towards all that were left—"are the angels. You sing 'Glory to God.'"

They were all placed now, all taking it with the intent solemnity of small children whose eyes see beyond physical things. Martin's cheeks were flushed—to him the group made a beautiful picture. Head on one side, he looked it over. One thing was missing.

Slowly, solemnly, Martin placed a chair near the Mother Mary, climbed on it, stood there, legs astraddle, arms outstretched. The children did not need to be told what he was, instantly they knew. Janet knew, too. He was the star.

"Sing!" Martin said. " 'Oh, come, all ye faithful—' "

Janet had no time to start them off together, Shepherds, Wise Men and angels burst into uneven song, all on different keys, some a few words ahead of the others.

> Oh, come, all ye faithful,
> Joyful and triumphant—

The door opened and Martin's mother came in. Janet felt cold inside, for Mrs. Kahn was Jewish. Perhaps she would not understand. How silly, of course she would!

The triumphant chorus went straggling on:

> Oh, come let us adore Him,
> Oh, come let us adore Him——

Mrs. Kahn sat down. Her eyes rested with affection and deep understanding on Martin.

The chorus straggled off, the song died away, but the children stayed in their places. Martin held his pose.

"Mother!" he said. "We're playing the Christmas story. And I am the star."

"It is very beautiful," said Mrs. Kahn gently. "And I can see the star shining."

The group broke up. Martin rushed to his mother, flung his arms around her. "I was a good star, mother. I shone and shone and shone——"

The next day when the children were busy on Christmas gifts for their parents, Mark had difficulties. Mark was a small, tough boy with the face of a prize-fighter. He was good at games, at building with blocks, but when it came to making things with paper and wood, his fingers were all thumbs.

The other children were making candlesticks, bags, pictures, with ease and facility. Martin was making himself a star costume, or what he considered to be one. But Mark sat gloomily by a blank piece of paper, crayons clutched in a grimy hand.

"I can't make them draw!" he sighed. "I want to draw my Mummy a Christmas tree."

Janet didn't believe in helping too much, but she directed verbally, line by line, the drawing of that straggly tree. And she held the pieces of wood together while Mark hammered them awkwardly into the semblance of a frame. Once or twice she wondered if it could be worth while, the effort was so great, the product so far below the general standard. But when it was finished, Mark thought it was perfect. So perhaps it was worth while after all.

Mark fought his tough, tempestuous way through the year. In the spring the children decided to dramatize Oscar Wilde's *Selfish Giant*. They chose their parts—all but Mark.

"Mark," said Janet, "are you going to be a child or a flower?" He had no dramatic talents; it was best to put him in a minor rôle.

"No," said Mark. "I am going to be Spring. You know— 'And the children came running into the giant's garden, and with them came the Spring.' "

"But," said Janet feebly, "Spring is always a girl. She wears a green dress—and flowers in her hair."

"She is going to be a boy," announced Mark firmly if confusedly, "because I am her."

During the week of preparation for the little play, Mark worked feverishly on the costume that he had designed for himself. He couldn't sew, therefore he cut a hole in a piece of green cloth, draped it poncho-fashion around him and anchored it with a green sash. After that he worked painstakingly to make a wreath of paper flowers, lop-sided little flowers smeared with paste. Worn slightly askew over his pugilistic face, the effect of the wreath was devastating. Janet held on to herself by sheer force of will. The children never smiled. To them Mark as Spring was entirely satisfactory, even beautiful.

The play went through without a hitch. A few mothers, Mark's not included, put their hands over their mouths when Mark, Spring in every inch of him, danced lightly in.

Two weeks later, Mark died of spinal meningitis. It was Janet's first experience of that hardest part of teaching—the death of a child one has grown to love. She went to the sad little funeral, but afterwards she couldn't go to see the father and mother—of that she was sure. Mark had been their only child.

But after a struggle with herself, she went. The apartment seemed very quiet. Mark's toys were piled neatly in a corner of the room and on the wall was his funny, pathetic Christmas picture. His father took it down, held it carefully in his hands.

"I wish," he said, "that you could help us find some way to keep this picture—it's almost all we have of Mark. Do you think if we used varnish that would make it last? The paper is beginning to crack. . . ."

So that was teaching! Laughter and heartache, rewards and disappointments, successes and failures. When summer vacation came, Janet was happier than usual to be going to the small, remote Canadian village where the last summers had been spent. The year had been so full of experiences that now she was going to give her emotions a rest. She could stretch out oɪ the warm sandy beach, soak in the sun and the salty air, bɛ nothing but a vegetable.

It was an excellent plan, but it didn't work. For in the second week there was the House.

Chapter
35

HOUSE FOR SALE

WALKING ALONG THE BEACH of the quiet little cove, Janet came on the house. There were only three houses built on a piece of rising ground above the beach and this was the middle one. It stood there, a trifle forlorn in its worn paint, its broken windows, with apple trees crowding around it as if to hide its shabbiness from prying eyes. A sign said FOR SALE.

Don't be silly, Janet said to herself, of course you can't buy a house. Houses are expensive. But she went in at the gate that hung loose on its hinges and up the path, through, the twisted apple trees to the house. The front porch had rotted away, but she managed to stand on a board and peer in the windows. And instantly she knew that this was her house, that she must have it. But of course it was quite out of the question.

Back at the farm, where she boarded, she asked Mrs. Ellwood about it. "Ralph Dakin's house? Oh, it's been empty for five years, ever since his mother died. Ralph wants to sell, and he isn't asking too much for it, there's no road to it, you see. You weren't thinking of buying it, were you?"

218

"Well, not exactly," Janet said. "But I'd like to know how much he's asking for it. Somehow I'm curious."

"I'll call him up. Can't do any harm."

When the telephone conversation was over, Mrs. Ellwood relayed the information to Janet.

"He says he's willing to sell it cheap."

"How cheap?"

"Well, it's not in such good repair, and he doesn't want to fix it himself."

"But—but—*how much?*" Janet's voice shook with eagerness.

Four hundred and fifty dollars. Cash."

Four hundred and fifty dollars! Four hundred and fifty dollars for a whole house! And she had five hundred dollars, the first royalties on her book. She felt as if an angel had leaned down from Heaven and put the house in her hand. Only, of course, it was the Publisher who had done that.

"I'll go down and see it," she said, knowing quite well that she would be willing to buy it without ever stepping inside. For when a house reaches out and says to one, "You belong to me," then everything is over. "Tell Ralph I'll meet him there if he'll bring the key."

When she got to the house, Ralph was waiting for her.

"It's a pretty good house," he said, as he put the key in the lock. "Only the boys broke the windows and it's got a bit damp inside. You'd have to have the porch repaired. And there ain't any water laid on."

As if that mattered! Janet stepped over the threshold into her house. There were two big living rooms, their faded paper showing the one-time splendor of a gold, scroll-like design. There were fireplaces in both rooms. On one mantel stood a shining metal plate saying in bright letters, TILL WE MEET AGAIN.

"How nice!" Janet said. "I'll put it on the front door. It sounds so cordial."

Ralph gave her a queer look. "Better not. That's a coffin plate. We used to take 'em off and keep 'em. Sort of souvenir of the departed. If I remember rightly, that was my Uncle Richard's."

"Oh!" said Janet, slightly chilled. She went on to the kitchen. There was a small stove still in place, its name in large, embossed letters was HOUSEHOLD PET. It had a cozy sound.

Upstairs there were three low-ceilinged bedrooms, two of them papered in a hideous, screaming red.

"Ma liked warm colors," Ralph explained, a trifle apologetically. "How does the house suit you?"

"It will do very well," Janet said with a casualness she didn't feel. "I'll take it."

There were all kinds of preliminaries to be gone through— the searching of the title, the signing of the deed, the payment —and the house was hers. Hers to renovate and furnish on a hundred dollars—she had saved a little extra.

Fifty dollars went to mend the porch and repane the windows. Fifty dollars left for furniture. Well—! She wouldn't be able to live in it this summer.

"Isn't it too bad?" she said to Mrs. Ellwood. "I do want to stay in it at least for a few days."

"What's preventing you?" asked Mrs. Ellwood. "Furniture? Heaven's sakes! Let's go up in the attic and see what I've got."

The attic produced a big double bed, a few chairs, some old dishes, a table somewhat wobbly in the legs, a Franklin stove.

"That's about all you want for a start. I'll have them taken down on the ox-cart. The stove's the most important thing; apt to be cold down there so close to the water."

There followed a week of violent activity, for there were things to be done inside the house. Newspaper that had been under the carpets had stuck to the floor and had to be scraped off. The bedrooms had to be repapered, the living rooms and kitchen would do. Janet went to the nearby town and bought rolls of paper, a pale green paper with little bouquets of flowers that made her think of an English garden. A local woman helped with the papering. Guests at the farm came down and helped, too.

When the upstairs was freshly papered and the floors scrubbed, the house seemed ready to live in. Other people came with offerings of a piece of furniture, a few dishes, and—this was only a loan—sheets, blankets. The most magnificent gift of all was a patchwork quilt. A washstand was made from old packing cases covered with oilcloth. The pitcher and bowl, covered with pink roses, Janet found in another attic. In the second bedroom the local carpenter built a bunk for a bed. Janet named it "the ship room."

To hide the miscellaneous finishes of chairs and table, she painted them all black. And what distinction black paint gave to a chair that had been golden oak! Never had a house been so adequately, so exquisitely furnished. There were large empty open spaces in the downstairs rooms, but those were to grow on. Upstairs the small flowery bedroom was homelike, the big bed with its patchwork quilt filling most of it. Frilly white curtains at the windows did a lot for the whole house.

She moved in on an evening when the fog was rolling up in banks, hiding the bay entirely, wrapping the land in a wet white blanket. Janet could almost feel the house shivering. She hurried to light a wood fire in the Franklin stove, and in the Household Pet. She wasn't alone, Louise, a young artist staying at the farm, had come down with her. It was Louise who had been the most help in getting the house ready—she had suggested painting the furniture black, had helped to paint it.

They sat by the fire after supper. The wood crackled cheerfully and the firelight danced on the walls, bringing out the remnants of gold in the wallpaper. Outside, the fog laid its cold white fingers on the windowpanes. There was something a little eerie in the blank whiteness outdoors, in the quiet of the house, and in the spaces where furniture should have been.

Going to bed was chilly, for there were not any stoves upstairs. Janet slept in the double bed, Louise in the bunk in the ship room. In spite of the chilliness, they were soon asleep.

Then the noises began. Footsteps pattered from one end of the house to the other. There were peculiar rumblings on the roof. It was more than eerie in the stillness, with the lapping of the waves between the mysterious sounds.

"Janet!" called Louise from her room. "Are you hearing things?"

"I certainly am."

"What do you think it is—"

"Oh, probably Mrs. Dakin's ghost. I had a sneaking idea she'd come back to look for that red wallpaper."

"Gosh!" Louise said. "I'm coming in with you." Wrapped in a quilt, she perched on the foot of Janet's bed. The rumbles continued, the footsteps went on pattering, there were mysterious creaking sounds.

"Joking aside," said Louise. "What do you think it is?"

"Squirrels," answered Janet. "They're in the walls. And the rolling sound is an apple falling on the roof."

"Very logical," Louise said. "But how do you explain the creaking?"

"I don't," said Janet. "But I think it's just the house. It's been cold and it's warming up. At least that *might* be it."

"I'm not so sure." Louise wrapped the quilt closer around her. "But I'm awfully cold and sleepy and I'm going back to bed. If Mrs. Dakin gets you in the night, just yell!"

"That is if I *can*," Janet said. "I've heard ghosts work swiftly and silently. And she might begin in your room. I believe she died there."

"Shut up!" Louise shivered. "Enough's enough." She shuffled back to her room. The noises stopped and it was quiet in the little house. Outside the waves still lapped softly on the beach.

Chapter
36
DECISION
—NOT MADE

As if the new house was not enough to keep her busy, the idea for another book came into Janet's mind. There was still a great deal to be done, one of the upstairs rooms to be papered, the kitchen to be made more workable. And here, in the midst of it all, came the book, nagging, insisting, nudging, in the way of unwritten books. So there was nothing to do but give the book its head. And, with paper spread out on the red-checked cloth of the table, Janet began to write.

This was to be a single story of the village and its children, not a collection of stories. The first few pages were rewritten many times; her standards were higher now. The children in this book must be alive, must be real children, as real as Martin and Mark. Not only the children but the village must go into it. The sea must be in it, too, must be in every page of it—the sound of the sea, the color, the smell of fish-nets drying, the taste of salt on the lips. But there were distractions. The village children coming to see the "pretty house." The local plumber wanting to know when she was planning to add a bathroom. Packages from the mail-order house arriving by wheelbarrow along the beach. She stopped writing to unpack a stiff-looking enamel pitcher and bowl for the ship room, saucepans for the eager top of the Household Pet. It was hard to get back into a writing mood, so she went outdoors and sat down under the apple trees, looking out across the calm blueness of the Cove.

It was then that she saw a man coming up the path. He didn't interest her especially. A tall man with a lean, sunburned face, not especially handsome, and, she judged, somewhat older than she was. When he stopped and looked down at her, his eyes were of a clear blue that was startling in his brown face.

"Pardon me," he said. "The tide has come up suddenly and I think I'm marooned. I don't seem to be able to get back along the beach. Isn't there a way to the village over the hill?"

"Yes," Janet said. "Through my back yard and up the path. I have to go that way myself when the tide comes in."

"Thank you," the stranger said, but didn't go. Instead, he sat down on the grass beside her.

"Quite a bit of English left in your talk. I'll have to stay and hear more of it. I was born in England, you see."

"Not much English left, now," said Janet. "Only the a's are

broad. And I'm going to be an American citizen soon." She had no idea what made her tell him this.

"Good for you, if you live there," he said. "I had a hard time making the grade. I'd get myself all worked up to it and then just couldn't haul down the old flag. Finally I did."

"I'm not going to. I'll just fly two flags together."

He looked at her quizzically. "You can't do that. It isn't done. One flag *has* to fly above the other. So you'd better be sure that you really want to make the change."

"Heavens!" Janet said. "How did we ever get into this conversation? I don't even know you."

"But *I* know *you*. I've watched you going along to your house. And—to be perfectly frank—I sat on the beach and *waited* for the tide to cut me off. Did I tell you that my name is Perry Arnold? I live in Boston."

The next afternoon he was back again. Janet showed him the house.

"It's charming," he said. "But it seems funny to think that you're planning to live here all alone."

"I have friends." Janet was stiff. "Plenty of them. And I think my mother is coming next summer."

"Oh, I've no doubt you have friends. But you're young to have a house of your own. I wondered——"

On the third day they went for a walk, a long walk through the woodland path that led to an inlet known as Deep Cove. The path was so narrow that most of the way they had to walk single file. The evergreen needles made a springy carpet underfoot, there was the spicy tang of balsam in the air. They stopped to pick the sun-warmed blueberries, to hunt for the small red bunchberries that hid with such cunning under their green leaves.

There were many things to talk about, many interests that they shared. Perry had grown up in Cornwall, he had played on the sands and had explored the smugglers' caves.

"Can't you just taste the clotted cream?" asked Janet. "And see those little cottages with their gardens?"

"And King Arthur's castle," said Perry. "Did you ever go there?"

"I never did. When I first came here I used to think that I'd left tradition behind in England. America seemed all newness and skyscrapers. But I found it wasn't so."

"No," said Perry. "I have found plenty of old-world atmosphere in Boston."

"And I've found it in New York. Since I've had Margaret Brooks for a friend she has shown me so many things. Do you know funny little Gay Street? Or MacDougall Alley? There are all sorts of queer little shops. Margaret took me to one that sold music boxes along with cheese and candy!"

"Sandy Cove is as different as anything I've seen anywhere," Perry said. "Some one should put it in a book."

"I have! In the book I wrote last year and in the one I'm writing now. It fits naturally into a book. Of course these are children's books and you wouldn't be interested."

"Why not? If I wrote I'd rather write for children than for grown-ups. Grown-ups read a book once—perhaps twice— children read it until it falls to bits!"

They were at Deep Cove now. On the rocks overlooking the inlet they sat for a long time talking, the feeling of companionship growing. Companionship and something more than that.

The homeward way was by the sea, over the gray rocks that tumbled in careless piles down to the water. It had been a long climb up the face of a particularly steep rock, and at the top they rested, looking out at the sea, watching it as it broke in ragged white lines on the shore. All at once Janet knew that Perry wasn't looking at the sea, but at her. Then his arms were around her and he was kissing her, not in the casual way that Stephen had kissed her, but with an intensity that startled her.

"Do you happen to know," he said, "that I love you very much?"

"But you *can't*. You've only known me three days."

"Long enough. I knew the first day. But I'm not going to ask you to decide anything now. It's too important a decision to be made quickly."

They went on in silence, because there seemed to be nothing more to be said. Over the rocks, along the road, through the village, along the beach, still in silence. At the gate she held out her hand. "You're going away tomorrow, aren't you?"

He nodded. "Yes, I have to get back to work."

"I'm sorry." He had both her hands now and he was drawing her closer to him. Then he kissed her again.

"Good-bye," he said. "Good-bye, my dear. It wouldn't be too much if I asked you to write to me? And next summer I'll be back. You can make your decision then." He started along the beach, then turned and looked back. "Let me know what you decide about the flags."

Very slowly, Janet went up the path to the house. Her half-finished book was on the table. This was her home and her book

—there were other kinds of happiness ahead. Perhaps there would be marriage, perhaps not. As Perry had said, it was too important a decision to be made quickly. And when she had made a decision before, it had not worked out very well. This time she must be careful. Strangely enough, she had almost forgotten about Stephen. With a sort of pride she realized that she hardly ever thought of him, and when she did it no longer hurt.

She sat down at the table and picked up her pen. For a long time she sat there, seeing Perry as he stood at the gate, seeing again his slightly crooked smile. She shook herself a little. Of course she was going to write! But she put the pen down again without writing a word. It wasn't quite as easy as that.

Chapter
37 *AMERICAN —VERY NEW*

THE BOSTON BOAT was coming into its North River pier. Janet, returning from Canada, stood on the deck looking up at the city skyline. It was a friendly skyline now; she knew every building, recognized even the big apartment houses. With a sudden shock she realized that although her house, her very own house, was in Canada, she was coming home. She knew then that she would never want to live, for any length of time, in any other country.

That feeling stayed with her as she went into another year of teaching. The big kindergarten room was well-known ground now; the blocks, the dolls, the toys, the pictures on the walls all were familiar. Only the children were new, crowding in with eager first-day faces, the boys looking a trifle sheepish, the girls pleased with themselves in their crisp, spotless dresses.

Again that feeling of belonging—how often was she to feel it? But Janet had to stop abstract thinking and get into action. Donald had climbed like a wild monkey to the top of the jungle gym from where he was spitting lavishly down on the heads of startled and enraged little girls. Roger, resenting his first separation from his mother, was clinging to the doorknob, kicking his feet against the door, shrieking like a steam-whistle. Bob, a painfully shy child, had retired under a table like a frightened rabbit. Janet found her hands quite full. They were literally full—of Roger, who, detached from the doorknob, was clinging frenziedly to both of them. She took him on her lap and he cried hot tears down her neck.

This group was a little more difficult than last year's, she decided. At least it was more noisy, and certainly as a whole they were more homesick and tearful. Would there be any children like Mark and Martin? she wondered. Or were they all just bits of restless activity?

It wasn't long before her question was answered. She had noticed a tall dark boy wandering vaguely around the room, not seeming to settle down to anything. Now she saw him curled into a ball in the windowseat. Going over she found that his eyes were closed, and by him was a sign, printed in straggly crayon letters:

PLEASE DO NOT DISTURB

She sat down beside him, wondering what approach to take. He opened his eyes and looked at her.

"They make a lot of noise," he said.

"But they're having such fun. What do you like to do, John? Play with blocks?"

"No."

"Draw pictures?"

"No."

"Well—what—"

John sat up. "I like to read books," he said. "Books like *The Wind in the Willows.*" His eyes were interested. "Have you ever been in England?"

"Yes, I lived there," Janet said.

Now his eyes sparkled. "I suppose if you lived there you know Rat and Mole really well?"

"I do." Janet was definite about it. "I know them—really well."

The year was not going to be dull after all!

When everything settled down, Janet found that this was an unusually intelligent group of children. They ate and drank stories. They snapped at information as a trout snaps at a fly. She had to be on her toes to keep up with them. On her toes and in the library looking up all kinds of answers to questions.

It was John who noticed that when she told them the story of the first Thanksgiving she said "your country."

"Isn't it *your* country, too?" he asked, looking at her in his queer, searching way.

"No," Janet said. "I'm not an American. At least not yet."

"Why?" asked John, bluntly. "Why not?"

Why indeed? Janet asked herself. She had grown to feel this was her country, her home. Why, then, did not she make it so in reality? She loved the country, the people, the way of living. So she wrote to Mother and Lawrence and they wrote back,

"Why not?" Mary was still at Columbia, working for a higher degree. Janet talked it over with her.

"The only thing that's really holding me back," Janet said, "is sentiment. I don't want to say, 'I renounce my allegiance to King George the Fifth.' Silly, isn't it? But every time I think of it I can see myself on Coronation Day, waving a little flag, shouting myself hoarse, and I can see the King and Queen in the royal coach *with their crowns,* real golden crowns! You'll admit a President, even in a top hat, isn't a fair exchange for a King."

Mary laughed. She had taken out her citizenship the year before. "You're a real Britisher! No one on the outside can realize what a hold the King has on one, however absurd and illogical it may be. It was easier for me, because I'd never been to England. It's only crossing the border for a Canadian."

"Well, I'm going to do it," Janet said. "I'm sure I want to, now." Perhaps the letter that had come from Perry that morning had something to do with it. His letters were different from any others. Worth reading from beginning to end. And at the end of this one he had said, "Are you any nearer to being a citizen? I'd like to feel we belonged to the same country."

A week later she went down to City Hall to take out her citizenship papers. All the way down she pictured the setting. It would be a handsome room, of course, with big windows— perhaps looking across to the Statue of Liberty. That was how it should be.

The vision was still with her as she stood in line waiting for admission to The Room. It was an oddly assorted crowd— women with handkerchiefs over their heads, an old Italian clutching a small American flag, a couple of Negroes, a French priest . . . the only common denominator the look of anticipation on their faces.

Then the doors opened—on a drab courtroom with high windows through which one could see only a patch of sky. Packed like sardines in a can, they stood or sat, and waited for the ceremony.

In spite of the lack of an appropriate setting, there was a thrill to it when it came. Janet was glad to find that the oath was a composite one. "I renounce my allegiance to King George of Greece, to King Albert of the Belgians, to the President of France, to George the Fifth, King of Great Britain and of the Dominions Beyond the Seas." That made it impersonal, one did not mind it.

The hands raised to take the oath dropped, individuals stepped forward to sign their names. A red-haired woman with a baby more carrot-topped than herself hesitated a moment, then plumped the baby into the arms of a surprised courtroom attendant, took the pen. The attendant, holding the baby awkwardly, gave a helpless look around him. A ripple of laughter began to go through the crowded room, grew and grew, rose to a roar. The woman finished signing her name, grinned at the crowd, turned to take her baby. He turned from his mother and hid his face on the man's shoulder. Laughter came in waves, beat on the dun-colored walls, rolled back again. The old Italian woman stepped forward and gave the baby her flag. He took it and looked it over, gravely. The judge rapped with his gavel. There was silence.

"You are now citizens of the United States of America. . . ."

They came out of the courtroom, these very new citizens, in a quiet mood. Outside, everything looked a little different.

Bowling Green, the Battery, the gray downtown buildings—these, Janet thought, are part of *my country*. There was, mixed with her feeling of pride, a loneliness, the loneliness of a newcomer who has stepped over the border of a strange land. She would have to write Perry; he would understand just how she felt—and he was waiting to hear her decision about the two flags.

It was late in the afternoon now, and she was to meet a group of her college friends at Washington Square—why the Square she didn't know. When she got there they were waiting and they handed her, solemnly, a large book in a homemade cover of red, white and blue. Janet read the title: GUIDE BOOK FOR A CITIZEN OF THE UNITED STATES OF AMERICA. She opened it and the first page informed her that here was the spot where Washington had cut down the famous cherry tree. The comfortable old Square was, she felt, laughing gently at the joke. The guide book, with its mixture of fact and highly inaccurate information, led them to the Treasury Building, a reminder that a citizen could pay taxes, and on to a place from which she could see the Statue of Liberty.

Dinner, so the guide book said, was to be at one of the oldest houses in New York, the Little House in Greenwich Village, a very old house which had stood there as the city grew up around it. Nothing could be more American than that. Laughing and hungry, they turned the knob on the door of the Little House. It opened, not on a scene that promised dinner, but on a comfortable, homelike living room, with a middle-aged man sitting by the fire, reading his paper.

"Can we have dinner here?" blurted Nancy, always the mouthpiece of the group.

The man looked her over, solemnly. "Not if I know it," he said.

"Isn't this a restaurant? Isn't it the Little House?"

"No, it isn't a restaurant now. It's a private house. In fact it's *my* house. I bought it last month."

"But—but—" Nancy stuttered. "We're sorry—but—you see—our friend here has just become an American citizen—we planned to celebrate——"

"Then you'll have to celebrate elsewhere," the man said shortly. "And would you mind shutting the door as you go out?"

On the sidewalk they stood and rocked with laughter.

"Oh!" said Nancy. "Will you ever forget his face? Come on, Janet, we'll have to find another place to eat. He doesn't seem to care that you've just become a citizen. We've been taking it for granted that every one was celebrating with us!"

So dinner was at the Hotel Lafayette, with good-natured teasing and laughter—and finally home to bed.

Alone in her room, Janet sat in the chair by the window. Thoughts were racing through her mind. For a little while sleep would be impossible. She was glad that her first day as an American had begun with serious thought and deep emotion, that it had gone out on a tide of friendliness and laughter. For those contrasts, to her, *were* America. As for one's other country, one didn't lose that, but kept all the remembered lovely things that had come to be part of oneself. Blackberry hedges, yellow of primrose woods, gold of prairie wheatfields, sheen of bamboo in moonlight, the scarlet flame of maples—these would now always be part of the same pattern, a pattern so blended together that one scarcely knew where one part left off and the other began. And, basically, her countries, old and new, believed in the same things, though there might be differences in speech and custom.

Even after she was in bed she lay there in the darkness, thinking. It had begun to rain and the patter of raindrops on the window took her back to the day when, through the pages of *Little Women,* she had met America for the first time. Somewhere along the road that led from the House on the Hill to the present, she had left the girl who was so unsure, so lacking in confidence, so afraid to try new things. America had had a great deal to do with the change—America and the people along the road. Suddenly the feeling of strangeness and loneliness was gone; she tucked the friendliness of her new country around her like a soft warm blanket. What the future held for her she didn't know. Of two things only she was certain. There would be children—her own or other people's—and there would be books.

NEWBERY AWARD BOOKS
AND NEWBERY HONOR BOOKS
AVAILABLE IN PUFFIN